For Karla, Cindy, and Aidan
and all the other girls
who have found
their voices.

Chapter 1

My father left home today. He walked into my bedroom carrying two suitcases, ones I'd never seen before, kissed me on the head and said, "See you next Sunday." He turned to leave then hesitated at the door, as if he realized he might need to give me some explanation. "I just can't keep living in this house, Jackie," he said, keeping his eyes on the floor. As if I couldn't have figured that out for myself! What I couldn't figure out was why, but it was a hard question to ask, especially since my father and I aren't exactly used to having heart-to-heart discussions.

As far as I can tell, he didn't say a word to my mother, who sat at the kitchen table the whole time he was leaving. He never said goodbye to her, nor she to him. They stayed at opposite ends of the house, repelling each other the way magnets do when they're turned backward.

From my bedroom window I watched him

throw his suitcases into the trunk of his car. Then he stood beside the open car door and waved up at me. I thought I saw him mouth the words, "See you soon." I raised my hand to answer back. Then he took off. I realized he hadn't even told me where he was going. Where does an adult run away from home to? If he were my age, he might end up downtown, living on Ste-Catherine Street, sleeping in doorways with a sign around his neck and a tin can at his feet. He might even get a dog. It seems to be the fashion nowadays with street kids. They tie red bandanas around their dogs' necks, then get the dogs to curl up on the sidewalk around the can of coins. I guess the animals help bring in more money.

Would my father simply go and live in his workshop? He owns a large loft down by the water in Lachine, and from there he runs his refurbishing business. I know there's a couch that he could sleep on in one corner. I've spent lots of time on it myself over the years, watching cartoons on the old boxed-in TV. He's also got a computer with Web hookups where I go to do a lot of my school projects. Would I still be able to do that?

Now, lying here on my bed, I'm trying hard to figure it out. I guess there were clues about my parents' unhappiness. For example, about a year ago they stopped talking at dinner. We all just sat shovelling the food that my mother had prepared into our mouths without looking up. Not that we've ever been the chattiest family on the planet.

Our conversations are usually short and full of one-liners, question-and-answer style. My parents ask each other things like, "Did you get that job done?" and "Did the hydro bill come in?" For me it's usually, "How was school?" or "Did you pass your test?" You see, nothing earth-shattering.

Also, one Saturday morning not long ago, I heard a big bang in the basement. I tiptoed down the stairs, hoping to find my old cat, Igor, returned safely home. He had disappeared a month earlier. But it wasn't Igor. It was my father, doing his own laundry. He was standing in the laundry room in his gray boxer shorts, shoving a great heap of clothes, darks and lights together, into the machine. He scratched his hairy belly and looked embarrassed when he saw me, so I pretended it was normal to see him down there, sparing us both the embarrassment.

But the biggest clue of all — the one that should've tipped me off — is that many times in the last few months I woke up to find my father asleep on the spare couch in our den instead of in the queen-sized bed he normally shares — or I guess I should say *shared* — with my mother. Those mornings, it was awkward sitting across from my mother at breakfast. She looked haggard, with dark, puffy bags under her eyes as though she hadn't slept. I probably should have asked her about it, but I really didn't know how to ask why my father no longer wanted to sleep in the same bed as her. I kept looking at the bags under her eyes. They seemed to be growing bigger by the minute, as though they were filling up. I read once in a magazine that you could freeze spoons and press them into your eyes to get rid of bags. Maybe I should have told her, but I didn't. It wouldn't have helped or changed things anyway.

The clock on my desk does its chirpy twelve o'clock chime, snapping me back to the present. My father's already been gone for three hours and I've been lying in bed thinking all this time. I have to talk to someone, so I call my boyfriend, Alex.

"Don't sweat it, Jackie. It's not that bad," he says. "Now that your parents've split up, you and your dad will probably do more stuff together than you did before. That's what happened to me." Alex's parents divorced when he was six. He can barely remember a time when they didn't live in separate homes, in different provinces. During the school year, Alex spends every second weekend at his dad's place across the border in Ontario. This summer, he'll be spending much of the summer there to help build a shed for his dad's carpentry business. Alex is incredible at building things. He's already won several miniature-bridge build-ing competitions around Quebec and wants to make it to the nationals by the end of next year, in Grade 10. He seems okay with his parents' situa-tion. I wonder if I'll ever get to that point myself.

After I hang up with Alex, I call my best friend, Katie. She says pretty much the same thing. Only, in her case, I can't figure out why. Her parents are still together and have been since high school. They're so lovey-dovey it sometimes makes me sick. They kiss every time one of them walks in or out of the front door. I guess when you have the model of a perfect couple in front of you every day all other couples seem doomed. So maybe my parents splitting up seemed inevitable to Katie.

"If your parents are miserable, this might help them get happy, and happy parents will make you happier, Jackie. Besides, you can use them to learn what not to do in a relationship, the same way I'm using mine to learn what to do." Katie's a person on a mission to have a wonderful life. She once told me that she feels she's on a fast train heading toward complete happiness and that all the things she has to deal with now, like school and parents, are just stations along the way. She says nothing is going to stop her.

"Don't let it get you too down, Jackie. Lighten up about it, okay?"

Katie is always trying to turn me into a more cheerful person. She thinks that because I'm not bursting out laughing every two seconds there must be something wrong with me, as if I have a blocked pipe in me somewhere.

"I'll try, but this isn't like some small insignificant thing you know, Katie. He is my father." I feel like Katie's acting like I've just told her something trivial, like my pet goldfish died.

"I know, Jackie. Look, we'll talk later, okay? I've got to go." Then she hangs up.

11

I don't know if I can be as cool about the whole thing as Alex and Katie want me to be. I mean it's like bang! Suddenly I've become one of those weekend kids, the kind you see at movies or McDonald's. I've always been able to recognize part-time dads by the way they seem nervous with their kids, the way they're always trying to catch up. I mean, it's only part-time dads who ask questions like, "So, how's school?" or "Did you win the basketball game?" in public. Come to think of it, those are the types of conversations I have with my father anyway. For example, he's met Alex a couple of times, but he's never asked me anything about him, as though that would be getting too personal. We stick to general stuff and I guess that isn't about to change.

I pull back the curtain to uncover my bedroom window again. It's past lunchtime and I'm not even dressed yet. I guess that's not so unusual, considering summer holidays started two days ago. I wonder if my father was waiting for me to finish Grade 8 before leaving home, as if leaving before then would have screwed up my exams. Could he have thought this through that deliberately? Had he been planning to leave for a long time or did he just wake up with a sudden urge to make today the day?

I sigh and lean on my windowsill, scanning our quiet suburban street. The only signs of life on this Sunday afternoon in June are twittering sparrows and squirrels darting frantically from tree to bush to tree. A few kids go by on bikes, towels rolled under their arms, heading to the local pool. An old man across the street is puttering in his flower bed, kneeling on one of those puffy garden pillows. I look at the house to his left and notice, to my surprise, that the sick girl is out on her front deck. She only comes out of her house a couple of times a year. I haven't seen her since last summer, and I'm glad, too. I hate it when she's outside. When she is, I try to avoid looking over there. I don't want her eyes to catch hold of mine, to see that I've seen her. I'm afraid she'll expect me to do something for her, to run across the street maybe, with a cure to her illness in my hands. I think sick people should stay indoors where they belong, tucked neatly between crisp, white sheets. They make me uncomfortable. Last year, I volunteered to be a candystriper at the Royal Victoria Hospital, which sits at the foot of Mount Royal downtown, sticking up like a giant Gothic castle. I thought it would be fun to get out of class one day a month. We had to wear goofy white uniforms with pink stripes and little caps stuck to our hair with bobby pins. We were supposed to smile a lot and ask patients if they needed anything, like water or magazines or pillow fluffing. It was basically our job to cheer them up, but I was hopeless at it. The sight of sick people lying so helpless, hooked up to tubes with brown liquid draining through them made me want to gag. I only lasted one day and spent most of it hiding out in the bathroom.

It seems like some sort of omen that the sick girl is standing outside on the very same day that my father leaves home. I watch her standing back in the shadow of her large front deck, as though the direct sunlight will melt her. The stone facade of her expensive house, the biggest one on our block, seems to be holding her up. Every time I've seen her she's stood the same way — perfectly still, her skinny arms stiff at her sides, as though she's been ordered to stand out there but can't get comfortable in the pose. Today she's wearing a short pink skirt and a white tank top and white sandals. Pretty fancy stuff for someone who's sick. But that's the way she always looks when she comes out, like someone who's waiting for a lift to a party.

In fact, the only time I've actually met the sick girl was at my tenth birthday party four years ago. My mother had insisted that I invite her because she was the new kid on the block. Her family had just moved in a few weeks earlier. I didn't want to invite her. I mean, who wants a stranger at their party? Plus, I knew she was sick even then, because I'd overheard some adults talking and I didn't want a sick person at my party. In the end, she just sat there, blending into the background. She didn't do anything fun, like take part in musical chairs, or throw water balloons, or put on some of the makeup that my friends and I had pooled into a basket. She seemed completely dull, so it was pretty easy to ignore her after that, which suited me just fine. But every now and then, when my mother sees the sick girl standing outside, she says, "It's a shame you never tried to become friends with her," as though that's the reason the sick girl looks so lonely over there and I could have tried harder at my tenth birthday party to include her.

Suddenly, the sick girl's mother opens the door and calls her inside.

I guess the lift to her party never came.

Chapter 2

"Jackie, now that your father's gone you and I will have to pull up our socks and do things for ourselves." My mother's telling me this as she washes a heap of dishes left over from last night. It's the first time she's mentioned my father since he left exactly one week ago, last Sunday.

"Like what things?" I ask.

"Like everything. We'll have to rely on each other." I guess that means I should grab a dishtowel and at least dry this load. So up I get. But I really don't know what "things" she means.

"Dad didn't do anything at home anyway," I say, attacking the stack of cutlery. I think I noticed a flinch in her face when I said the word "dad." But she doesn't respond. Instead, she turns on the hot water tap full force and rinses a plate as though she's trying to drown it. I wasn't lying when I said that my father didn't do much around the house. He left for work around seven-thirty every morning and often didn't come home until six-thirty. After dinner, he'd sit in his lounge chair and watch TV while my mother washed dishes and talked to her sister on the phone. Most evenings I'd vanish into my room to listen to CDs. I don't see how my father's leaving is going to change any of that.

As for tasks around the house, the only one that is now uncovered is recaulking the skylight once every five years — I was nine the last time he did it, and four the first time. Both times it was my job to steady the long ladder he had to climb. The first time around I barely reached the third rung. When I was nine I reached the fifth. I guess I won't find out how far up I reach this summer. Cleaning up the mess of tools and scraps of material in the garage from his reupholstery business was also an annual job for my father. But a few days ago, I went into the garage to grab my bike and discovered that his stuff had been cleared out. When I saw the nearly bare garage I gasped. It was like we'd been robbed. All he'd left behind were a few boxes of junk, two old bikes, and our lawn-mower, which I guess he wouldn't need since he was now living in an apartment. Not that he ever mowed our lawn much anyway. My mother usually did it. And she and I took turns putting out the garbage and recycling, too.

It occurs to me now that my father must have waited until he knew I wouldn't be home to clear out his stuff, so I wouldn't catch him in the act of further separating himself from us. I wonder if my mother was home when he did it, and if she was, how did that feel? It would have been hard to hear him banging around in the garage, which was separated from the kitchen by a pretty thin wall. Maybe she went into the den and blared the TV to drown him out. Maybe she just stood there and watched him. Who knows?

"Thanks for helping, Jackie," my mother says, trying to smile at me, when I've put the last dish away.

"Mom," I say, hanging the soaking dishtowel on the rack. "What happened?"

My mother's face folds, collapsing like a chair with broken legs. I'm afraid she might start crying. I wish I hadn't asked.

"It's complicated, Jackie. I'm not sure if I can tell you. I'm not sure if I even know myself. People grow apart. It happens when you're not looking." Then she heads for the phone. I know she'll be calling her sister, who's probably gotten a lot more of the real story than I'm ever going to get.

I could try asking my father the same question, if I ever see him again. He was supposed to pick me up this morning, but he called to say he needed to get his new apartment in order first. He promised we'd do something next Sunday. What could I say?

* * *

18

On Monday, my mother floors me by announcing that she has found work. Without telling me, she had put up a sign at our local depanneur, advertising her services as a housecleaner.

"I've got two clients already, Jackie. Isn't that great?" she says.

"Clients?" I respond, "Isn't that what lawyers have? Not maids." My mother just shoots me a hurt look that leaves me tongue-tied.

On Tuesday morning I watch her walk down the street after breakfast, carrying a pail full of cleaning supplies wearing jeans and a T-shirt, a pair of old running shoes on her feet. She's actually whistling, as if she's happy. She has to walk because my father took the car. The houses in this neighbourhood are pretty spread out, not like in some suburbs that are all made up of row houses. It isn't the type of neighbourhood where you can walk around carrying a pail and not get noticed.

"That wasn't so bad, Jackie," she says when she comes home later that afternoon. "And look at this, one hundred dollars for two houses." She slaps the money onto the kitchen counter like a poker player slamming down a bet. "Not bad for a day's work, I'd say."

"I guess," I respond. I don't sound very enthusiastic, but she doesn't seem to notice. She's smiling and her face is full of colour, probably from all the hard work. Her blue eyes look clearer today than they have for a while. The wrinkles around them are still there, but somehow, they've faded a bit.

By the end of the week, she's worked every day and I still haven't had the nerve to ask which houses she's cleaning. She's up to five clients now. What if some of her appointments, as she likes to call them, are at the houses of kids I go to school with? I'm thankful that it's summer and I can choose who I see. But if she is cleaning some of my classmates' houses, they'll tease me mercilessly once September hits. I can already hear the taunts: "Jackie, our toilet's dirty. Send your mommy over," and that kind of thing.

"Are you going to clean houses forever, Mom?" I ask her while we're eating. It's the first time I've made supper completely on my own. Nothing fancy, just spaghetti with store-bought sauce. My mother told me last night that it would be nice if I did this every now and then. She's really tired when she gets home. "Aren't you ever going to try to do something else?" When I was little, my mother worked as a nurse's aide. I think knowing that was what inspired me to try candy-striping.

"Can't you get work in a hospital again, like you used to?"

"Oh my God, Jackie, that was ages ago. I'd have to retrain. So much has changed in ten years. I don't even know if I'd still be qualified. So for now I have to do this," she says. "There isn't anything else I can do to make money. Besides, you like to eat, don't you? You like to have a place to sleep, don't you? You like..." and she continues with the long list of things I like until I yell, "Okay, I get the point!" Then she shuts off faster than a light, forgetting that I'm here altogether.

I don't tell Katie a thing about my mother's new job when I go over to her house to say good-bye on Saturday. She wouldn't be impressed. Katie likes to aim for the top, and cleaning houses isn't at the top of any wish list. Katie's off to live with her aunt in Nova Scotia for a whole month.

"My cousins told me to pack a bit of everything — beach wear, hiking gear, warm clothes for cold nights at the beach, and a whole load of party clothes. I think they have something planned for every day of the month." I watch Katie pack her party clothes with extra care. They're all kind of tight and sparkly, the kind of stuff I'd look really stupid in but makes Katie shine. Katie is tall and slim and she has naturally curly, reddish-blond hair that literally bounces on her shoulders, like a model's in a shampoo commercial. She's so excited. She hasn't asked me a single question about my parents and I don't want to spoil her good mood by bringing the subject up.

"Wow! That sounds great. You're lucky," I say, trying my best not to sound envious. I doubt I'll make it to a single party this summer, not with Katie gone.

"See you in August," she says, standing in her doorway as I'm leaving. "Don't forget to have some fun." She crosses her brows and fixes me with a harsh stare. I guess Katie knows me. She knows that without her around to motivate me, I'll probably just let fun slip by. She's kind of like the cheerleader of our group. With her gone, I probably won't even see any of the others. Katie's the glue that holds us together. Without her, I know I'd never be part of the group anyway. She's the one who pulled me in and kept me there. The other girls only acknowledge me through my association with her, as though she's the sun that's necessary just to turn me into shadow.

"Don't let the crap between your parents ruin your summer, okay?"

I nod ferociously. "Sure … at least, I'll try not to." So that's what's between my parents — crap. I thought there was nothing between them but empty space, especially after my mother's reference to them growing apart. Even when she said it, all I saw was space, wide open space, as flat and vast as a prairie.

Chapter 3

"There's someone I want you to meet today, Jackie," my father says when I'm settled into the passenger seat of his car Sunday morning. "Did you bring your bathing suit and stuff like I asked?" I nod.

I thought it was weird when he called last night and said he wanted to take me to Long Sault beach. I couldn't imagine going to the beach alone with my father. I guess we won't be alone, though. "Who is it?" I ask. I can't remember my father ever having a friend, someone he'd do stuff with, like watch hockey or go out for a beer. He just isn't that type of person.

"Her name's Nicole."

"Oh." I don't know what to say. I thought he meant a guy, a new friend, maybe another single dad that he was chumming around with. I never imagined it would be a girl. I don't have the nerve to ask if she's a girlfriend. How could my father have a girlfriend so fast? And guys who look like my father don't have girlfriends. They have wives who look like my mother, with graying hair. My father is almost bald, and I've seen him leaning over the sink to trim his nose hair.

We drive into the city along the highway, cross some of its concrete arches over container yards, and end up in Verdun, an old part of town that I've never been to. The houses here are tall brick buildings, with twisty, black staircases clinging to their fronts.

"She's an artist," my father says as we wind down a street that runs parallel to the St. Lawrence River.

"An artist!" I exclaim. He might as well have said she was a stripper. I can't imagine my father with an artist. My mother's only artistic talent is arranging her spice jars so that the colours match.

"I met her when I went into her shop to get this." My father lets go of the steering wheel for a few seconds and pulls up the sleeve of his T-shirt. A tattoo of a Ford Model T is sitting on his right arm, just below his shoulder. My father has a passion, an obsession my mother used to call it, for cars, old and new. But not in the way you'd think. He doesn't care about their motors; he's interested in their interiors, in the upholstery, because that's his job. He works refurbishing the seating on just about anything that moves — cars, trains, airplanes. Once, he even redid a yacht from Long Island that was docked in Montreal. It had *Rock-a-Fella* painted on the side.

"Is that what you meant by an artist? A tattoo artist? I thought you meant a painter."

"Same thing, don't you think?" my father says as he pulls up to the curb of a duplex. He gets out and I follow him up a winding staircase to the second-storey flat. A hand-painted sign in the window says *Tattoo Heaven* in red lettering inside a white cloud.

My father and Nicole kiss when she opens the door. I look across the street at the water so that I don't have to watch. I've never seen my father kiss anyone before, not even my mother. Well, unless you count a little peck on the cheek. But this is different. This is a real kiss, where the two sets of lips disappear inside each other. Then my father points to me and says, "This is Jackie."

Nicole holds out her hand. "*Enchantée*," she says. Then she turns to my father and adds, "She is very pretty, your little girl." My father just smiles at her, as though the compliment reflects more about her than me. I'm too stunned to respond. Nicole is way younger than my dad. She has long blond hair and is tall and slender. She's wearing a red bikini top and a long wraparound skirt in a wildflower print. On her head is a straw hat with pink-and-blue ribbons wrapped around the middle.

"She's also very shy, your little girl," Nicole says. She runs her fingers through my long black hair as she speaks, as though she's combing it. "What do you have to say?"

"Not much," I respond, shrugging my shoulders. I'd like to say that my father could have warned me about all this. I'd been picturing him all pathetic and lonely in his new basement apartment, looking out the tiny window as anonymous feet walked by. But the whole time he's been up here in Tattoo Heaven.

"We should get going," my father says. He picks up Nicole's beach bag and we head back to the car. I climb into the back seat without saying a word. I think about how I wish Alex were here, but he was at his father's when I called him last night to see if he wanted to join us. So, it's just me and my father and Nicole, alone for a whole afternoon. I stare straight ahead the whole way there, feeling like I'm at a movie. Nicole and my father have the starring roles. I watch the way their hands intertwine over the stick shift, the way they turn to look at each other every few seconds. I see their mouths moving in speech and opening wide to laugh, but I don't hear any words or sound. I'm blocking it all out. It's an old silent film, one that I wish I had a remote control to switch off. The proof that they're part of a movie is that they are completely unaware of me. They don't look back once. I'm just the audience, completely invisible.

About an hour later, our tires crunch over thick gravel in the parking lot, snapping me out of my reverie. "*Voila*, we're here," Nicole announces, finally turning around to flash me a brilliant smile.

I try to smile back, but my cheeks have gelled.

We set up our blankets and beach umbrella on a stretch of sand halfway between the water and a field that is dotted with picnic tables. The beach is pretty crowded. Summers in Montreal are short, so people take advantage of good weather. It's like we have two months in which to release all our outdoor energy before the temperatures start to fall, hitting rock-bottom lows of minus twenty-five in January. I'm surrounded by families and groups of teenagers, all lathered in sunscreen. There are beach volleyball and badminton games going on all around me, and the wide river is full of swimmers.

"Are you coming in the water?" Nicole asks me. My father is standing beside her. They're obviously both anxious to cool off.

"No, I'll stay here," I respond. I settle into the reclining chair and pull out the *I7 Mag* I grabbed before leaving home. I pretend to read, and watch them over the top of the pages. They're helping each other put sunscreen on. They're touching each other's arms, backs, and thighs. It's as though Nicole has injected some kind of magic potion into my father's newly stained skin. I've never seen him act this way before. Even Alex doesn't touch me like that, especially not in public. If he did, I think I'd die.

Two seconds later the two of them are racing through the sand to see who can get to the water first. I watch as my father lifts Nicole in his arms, scooping her up like a kid and dunking her down in the choppy St. Lawrence River water. I have a sudden sharp memory of him doing the same thing to me when I was little. I can even hear myself shrieking. I also remember the time a leech attached itself to my ankle at this very same beach. My father was carrying me back to our spot and my mother was running up and down, asking people if they had some salt. Later, he held my foot still while my mother drowned the creature in the white substance. It eventually shrivelled and let go enough for my father to yank it off.

When they come back, they collapse onto the large colourful blanket Nicole has spread in the sand. As the two of them lie there cooing, I try to figure out what Nicole sees in my father. He's forty-five and his belly hangs over the rim of his bathing trunks. It's not as disgusting as some beer bellies, the kind that jut straight out and make men look nine months pregnant. But someone like Nicole looks like she'd only go out with a guy with a six-pack. One thing I'll give my father is that his arms are pretty muscular. I guess that's because of the work he does. It's very physical. I've seen him carry large rolls of leather that must weigh a hundred pounds and sling them onto his work benches at his shop. On the other hand, he's pretty bald. Right now, his dome is shining in the sun. Nicole doesn't seem to mind any of this. In fact, at the moment she's tracing the line of hair that runs over his belly.

"I'd like to do a snake here," she says, "winding up over your chest and then dipping down." She stops at the band of his shorts. I think I might be sick.

"*Et toi?* You?" she says, looking up at me. "You must let me do a rose or a butterfly or something sweet on you."

I don't know what to say. I've never actually seen anyone get a tattoo. I've only seen the process in movies. The needles look like torture instruments. I picture them sinking deep into my flesh and drawing blood.

"I don't know," I reply.

"Your daughter doesn't know if she wants a tattoo," Nicole tells my father who's lying on his stomach with his hands folded under his face.

"Her mother would kill her anyway," he says. Although this is probably true, it hasn't even occurred to me. It's more the thought of Nicole piercing her permanent mark onto me that I'm uncomfortable with. It'd be like getting branded, like Nicole would own me afterward. Would that be fair to my mother? After all, she's had me for fourteen years; I've only known Nicole for a couple of hours. My mother has no idea about Nicole, or at least I don't think she does.

"Well, if you change your mind little girl, just let me know," Nicole says, stretching out beside my father, who has flipped onto his back. Nicole nestles her chin into the hollow between his neck and shoulder.

Watching them, I can't help thinking about me and Alex. Sure, we've held hands and necked, but not much more. Not that Alex doesn't try. The last time we were together, he unhooked my bra under my T-shirt. We were sitting in the back yard, on the old swing that my mother says someone is going to break their neck on, the boards are so rotten. I was terrified she was going to look out the kitchen window and see us, but Alex said not to worry, it was too dark.

In a way, I'm kind of glad now that he wasn't able to join us. If he were here and we were doing stuff together with my father and Nicole, we might end up looking kind of pathetic by comparison. As if they were the teens and we were the adults.

* * *

"What did you do with *him*?" my mother asks that night when I get home, spitting out the word "him." I've turned a light brown in the sun. It must be obvious that we were outside somewhere. I never mentioned the beach to her before leaving. I didn't know if I should.

"Nothing. We just hung out," I reply. I can't bring myself to tell her about Nicole. There's no way I could tell her about our day at the beach and flatten it in a way that would satisfy her. On the way home I thought about how, when I was little and the three of us did stuff together, we'd play and laugh the way my father and Nicole did today.

But that was years ago. We had long ago stopped going on family picnics or holidays. I remember my mother saying that she didn't know how to explain what went wrong with her and my father. The silence had just creeped in, little by little, over the years. Maybe my father needed Nicole to take him back to when he was younger and more care-free. My mother couldn't do it. She's the same age as my father and she often looks it, too. Her hair is short and frizzled from too much hair dye, and her face is saggy. She used to be really pretty, though. I can see it in old pictures.

"He gave me this for you," I say. Before letting me out of the car my father had pulled an enve-lope out of the glove compartment.

"Give this to your mother," he said. He didn't look me in the eyes when he said "mother." We had-n't said two words to each other the whole way back from Nicole's. I remembered that I'd thought of asking him what happened, the same way I'd asked my mother. But the timing just didn't seem right.

"I hope you had a good time today," he said finally.

"Oh, I had a blast," I snapped. I can't believe how clueless my father is. How could he think I'd enjoy watching him and Nicole flit around like a couple of lovebirds all day?

"You'll like Nicole when you get to know her."

"Sure, Dad," I replied. I know I should have said more than that. I should have told him that he should have told me about her first. I should have told him he had no right to be so happy when my mother obviously wasn't. But then I saw the curtain in the porch move and I knew that my mother was watching us. At that moment, I just wanted to get out of the car.

"I'll pick you up next Sunday," my father called as I slammed the car door. I didn't bother to answer.

Now, I watch my mother open the envelope. It's full of money, a thick wad of ten- and twenty-dollar bills. My mother flicks the money with her index finger, fanning it. Then she sticks the envelope on top of the fridge.

As she walks away, I think of my father, exchanging me and my mother for Nicole. And then giving us money to make up for it.

The only bright side I can think of is that maybe my mother can now give up housecleaning. We won't need the money all that badly.

Chapter 4

I'm lying on my bed the next day, listening to the
Black Eyed Peas, thinking about my day at the
beach, when the doorbell rings.

I hear the voice of a woman that I don't recognize talking to my mother at the front door,
followed by footsteps down the hall to the living
room. I wait a few minutes, then follow them, stopping at the doorway. I poke my head around the
frame and see that it's the mother of the sick girl.
She doesn't look like she has a sick daughter.
That's because she is so well-dressed and so neat
and tidy, you'd think she only has herself to look
after. She looks the way anchorwomen do — a
two-piece suit with a pretty brooch on the lapel, her
hair perfectly styled and turned under at her chin,
blush, eyeliner, and lipstick in all the right places.

She and my mother are sitting on the sofa while
the sick girl's mother is telling her story. I pull
back and listen from the hallway, where I can't be

seen. She is saying that her hands are full with doctor's appointments and endless hospital visits, and that her daughter, Theresa, is going through a bad patch at the moment.

"I barely have time to brush my teeth," she says. "Let alone clean my house." I gasp. "You have no idea how important it is that I keep Theresa's environment spotless. She is so susceptible at the moment. Her immune system is way down. It's the chemo." I hear my mother tut. "So, I was wondering if you would consider becoming our housekeeper? I really need someone to come in every day. I'll pay you well, of course." The sick girl's family must have money because they own the biggest house on our block and have two brand new cars in their driveway.

I hold my breath, praying my mother will say no. She can't have lost all her senses. I wonder how the sick girl's mother even knew that my mother cleans houses. Is it that obvious? Do all the neighbours stand at their windows to watch her walk by with her supply pail?

A minute later I hear my mother's voice, "Oh, I'd love to Mrs. Desjardins." I can just picture her holding her right hand to her chest, above her heart, she sounds so thrilled. I haven't heard her sound this excited in ages.

"Fantastic. I was hoping you'd say yes, Mrs. —" I hear my mother cut her off, as if she doesn't want to hear the sound of her own last name. "Please, call me Claire."

I haven't heard anyone use my mother's first name in ages. It's hard for me to think of her as Claire. And I don't think I ever even knew what the sick girl's last name was.

"All right. Thanks again, Claire."

"I'll have to tell my current clients that I can't work for them anymore. I'll call them tonight and start at your place tomorrow if you like."

"Fantastic. Now, as far as salary goes…"

Then I tune out. I can't believe that my mother has just become the housekeeper for the sick girl across the street. As if what she was doing before wasn't bad enough. An image of my mother standing over the sick girl's toilet, scrubbing away her sick germs, pops into my head. Beside it, I see the image of Nicole throwing her long blond hair back before doing a perfect cartwheel in the sand. My father stands beside her, clapping.

Nobody will be clapping for my mother as she performs her miracles of toilet transformation. I don't understand my mother. Why would she want to do this? Her husband of seventeen years has just left her. Shouldn't that make her want to do something to win him back? Maybe if she tried harder, got her hair done and lost weight. Worked at it a little. How is cleaning a sick girl's house going to make her look better?

"…and then we'll see how it goes," the sick girl's mother says.

"That sounds perfectly fine to me. I've often thought about Theresa and wondered how she was doing," my mother says. That's news to me. "It can't be easy for you."

"No, of course not. Theresa got sick when she was ten, just before we moved to this street. We used to live in a small town in the Gaspé. My husband and his brother run a small airline, regional flights into Quebec City and Montreal, some up to northern Quebec. They also get a lot of business from hydro workers, going back and forth into James Bay. He spends a lot of his time going back and forth now, but we had to make the move. There were no really good hospitals nearby, not for something like this. The Montreal Children's Hospital had a great reputation for dealing with kids with cancer."

Cancer! I never really thought too hard before about what kind of illness the sick girl had. I knew it was bad, but I never thought it might be life-threatening.

"Theresa's on her second round of chemotherapy. She's had chemo three years ago and actually went into remission for a while. We were so hopeful, we even thought of moving back because our families are all in the Gaspé, but then the cancer came back. This time, it's hit her a lot harder."

There's a long silence in the room. I think about the ten-year-old Theresa who was at my birthday party. She was thin and pale. She didn't even want any cake.

Now I guess I know why.

Chapter 5

Alex is back from Ontario, but he isn't staying long. He just came to pick up some more of his stuff. I go over to see him after lunch on Friday. When I describe Nicole to him, he says he can't wait to meet her.

"She sounds hot," he says.

"She's okay," I respond. I regret making my description so vivid. He's practically drooling.

"How long did you say her hair was?" he asks. I point to my waist. "Way to go for your father!" Alex laughs. Now I really regret telling him. I feel a pang of guilt about my mother. Alex is acting like my father's just traded in his old car for a better model. I think of pictures I've seen of my mother when she was younger. She was really pretty back then. The picture I like best is the one of her graduating class at college, where she studied to be a nurse's aide. She and all the others, mostly girls, are dressed up in white dresses with little nursing caps clinging to their bangs. She has a wide smile on her face and an eager expression.

We're sitting on Alex's bed listening to Eminem. Alex loves rap. Sometimes, he'll lip-synch along with the music, doing all the rap gestures, like grabbing his crotch. It's completely gross. My friends all think Alex is what they call drop-dead gorgeous. Every girl in my grade has had a crush on him at some point. I'm still not completely sure why he chose me, especially since I'm one grade below him. Plenty of girls his own age would jump at the chance to be his girlfriend. We met in band at school. I play the flute, he plays the saxophone. We ended up beside each other on a long bus ride back from a band competition in Toronto in the spring and he asked me out after that. I was totally surprised. It's not like I dazzled him with witty conversation the whole time. I'm usually pretty quiet, and I was especially quiet that day because the bus ride made me nauseous. And I don't think I'm exactly a knockout. I have shoulder-length dark hair, stick-straight and parted in the middle, and my eyes are light green. But I think my nose is way too big and my mouth is too small. I've actually measured it and it's only four centimetres long, maybe five when I'm smiling. Still, Alex seems to find me pretty enough to go out with.

"So, when am I going to meet this new girlfriend?" Alex bends close to me and tries to kiss me. I have a creepy feeling that he's seeing his version of Nicole as his lips touch mine.

"Quit it," I say, pushing him back. I know I should let him kiss me. It's not like it would be the first time. It's just that I keep replaying scenes from the beach in my mind. All I can see is my father and Nicole fooling around on the beach blanket. For some reason it makes me shy. I can't help wondering what Nicole would do in a situation that made her feel shy, but it's hard to imagine her being shy in the first place. In high school, she was probably the type of girl who knew how to get exactly what she wanted and never let anyone pressure her. She'd be the one calling all the shots. There's a bunch of preppy girls like that at my school. They look so cool and above everything. They walk with their heads up high and they're always dressed in tight clothes that show as much skin as the school will allow. It would be totally amazing to be that kind of girl, but I know I never will be. Whenever I'm with Alex, I feel nervous because he always wants to try things that I don't feel ready for. It's not that I don't feel anything when we fool around, 'cause I do. It's just that I always have the sense that Alex is planning his next move. His hand will be creeping up my leg. It makes me all tingly, but scared at the same time. Sometimes I think I made a mistake going out with a fifteen-year-old guy, who's almost sixteen, when I'm only fourteen. I had just turned fourteen, too, when Alex asked me out. In a way, he's closer to two years older than me.

Alex gets up to work on the model bridge he's trying to finish before leaving.

"How long are you going for this time?" I ask.

"At least two weeks. We got a lot to do."

"That's a long time," I say, but part of me is glad. The last few times we've been together he's made it pretty clear that he wants to do it. He doesn't say it in so many words, but whenever he gets the chance he always talks about other people doing it. I bet he's even thinking about my father and Nicole doing it. If he says anything out loud about that I'll really flip out.

I watch him pick up a toothpick, dip it in a pot of glue and twist it so that the glue spreads evenly around the tip. Then he does the same to the other end. He works slowly and delicately. Then he adds the toothpick cautiously to his creation, a flat bridge that so far looks a lot plainer than any of the others. I look around his room at all of his incredible bridges. They span the desktops, beautiful, delicate arches.

Alex adds a whole row of toothpicks to his new bridge, then stands back to admire his work.

"I gotta let that dry now. Anyway, I should pack. My dad'll be here soon." He opens his drawers and throws stuff out of them onto his bed. A heap begins to form right beside me.

"What d'ya think of these, Jackie?" Alex asks, holding up a pair of black boxers with a happy face on them and big hole cut out where the nose should be.

"Spectacular," I say, rolling my eyes.

"I thought you'd like 'em," Alex says. He stuffs

his clothes into two bursting gym bags. Then he sits beside me on his bed. "So, what do you want to do while we're waiting?" he asks, winking. This is the first time I've seen Alex since my parents separated three weeks ago. I thought I'd talk to Alex about all the changes in my life. I even pictured myself telling him about my mother's new job at the sick girl's house, but Alex is acting as though my life is still exactly the same. Besides, it's clear from his face that he has only one thing on his mind.

"Remember how far we got last time I saw you?" he asks, smiling. "In your back yard?" I nod. "I was hoping we could do that again." Alex traces a line from my neck down to my belly button, as though he's planning a bridge that would span the two body parts. All I remember about that night was wishing he hadn't taken my bra off so close to home.

Alex's hand is under my T-shirt, inching its way up, tickling my belly. He's getting awfully close to his target when his mother calls upstairs, telling him his dad is here. He yanks his hand out and gets up off the bed. It's like a light going off. "Well, if you guys do go back to Long Sault, call me at my dad's. He's not far from there. I'll have him drive me over. I want to check that Nicole out for myself."

I nod and reach over and kiss him on the mouth. I can't have him going away thinking I'm a complete drip.

* * *

When I get home, my mother is crashed out in my father's lounge chair. She's just come back from the sick girl's house. She's been cleaning it for four days. By now, I know what type of cancer she has — leukemia. How could I not know? It's all my mother seems to want to talk about.

"The treatments are killing her," she says. "She came back this morning and spent the rest of the day throwing up. And do you know she has lost all her hair, poor thing? Just imagine losing all your hair at your age?" I know my mother wants me to say something sympathetic, but I can't. The girl across the street is still like an apparition to me, she isn't real. I can't get all worked up about her like my mother can.

"Just imagine if you couldn't go out and visit your friends like you did just now, Jackie. How would you like that?" I'm surprised my mother even remembered that I was at Alex's. "Don't you know how hard it must be for her?"

"No I don't, actually. How could I?" I respond. I wonder why it's so important to my mother that I show some sign of concern for the sick girl. What does it matter to her? She's totally unaware of how disgusting I find it when she cleans over there. When I imagine her dusting, I see a million dust-coated germs rise in a puffball around her face. I picture her in the bathroom, elbow deep in the sick girl's toilet, the germs penetrating her yellow rubber gloves. To imagine her actually inside the sick girl's room brings the stench of vapour rub and antiseptic into my nostrils. And the thought of my mother mopping up the sick girl's vomit and sweeping up her fallen hair totally grosses me out. Just thinking these thoughts makes me shudder. My mother opens her eyes just in time to catch me.

"Oh, really! You can be so unfeeling, Jackie. You could try to put yourself in her shoes. It wouldn't be hard. You're the same age, you know. In fact, the poor girl could use a friend. She's totally cut off. I might bring you over there with me one morning. It wouldn't do you any harm to realize how lucky you are."

Lucky? My dad's gone. My mother seems to feel more for a stranger than for me. My stomach is growling with hunger and my mother isn't making any signs of getting up to make supper. I suppose I'll have to do it again.

This isn't my idea of lucky.

Chapter 6

On Sunday my father picks me up at ten again. He didn't call last night to tell me to pack beach stuff, so I assume we're not going to Long Sault today. In fact, I have no idea where we're going. Maybe he's going to show me his new apartment in Lachine. All I know about it is that it's in the basement of a large apartment building, close to his shop. But soon we're on the highway, retracing the route along the ribbons of concrete into Verdun. Obviously, we're going back to Nicole's.

"Ah, you brought your little girl to help I see," says Nicole, ushering me into her flat with her arm around my shoulder. I just look up at my father.

"Help what?"

"We're redoing Nicole's shop — Tattoo Heaven," my father says.

"Do you want to see?" Nicole asks. I just shrug and she leads me there, her arm still around my shoulder. Doesn't she think I can walk by myself?

Her shop is in a large room off the kitchen in the back of the flat. All the stencils have been pulled off the walls, leaving faded squares in the blue paint. But one wall is newly painted bright red. The upholstery has been ripped off her two dentist-like chairs, exposing the springs and frame. My father is refurbishing them with some beautiful calf's leather left over from an old job, dyed a deep tomato red.

"Your father, he has a talent for decorating, you know?" Nicole says to me. I raise my eyebrows. You'd never guess that from our house. The only painting up on our walls is a picture of some country scene, with hills and a river, that my mother bought at a flea market.

"It's true," Nicole continues. "Look what he's doing my chairs." We watch my father stretching out the leather and measuring and cutting. "I have to continue to paint. You can help if you want or you can watch. Or, you can go do whatever you want in my place. Don't be shy," Nicole says, picking up her roller and dipping it in a tray of deep red paint. I notice that even the ceiling has been painted red.

"Do you like it?" she asks me.

"It's nice," I say.

"Your little girl thinks it's nice," Nicole calls out to my father, as though she needs to translate what I say for him.

"That's good," he says. He has to concentrate because he's using the hot-glue gun. "We need to let this set for a while." He's working without his shirt on and I can see that the Model-T is no longer

his only tattoo. He now has some medieval looking symbol sprouting on his left shoulder. If Nicole
asks me if I like that I'll have to lie. It looks like it
could be a battle prop from *Lord of the Rings*. I've
never thought of my father as the warrior type.

"Oof! *Je suis fatiguée*. I'm so tired," Nicole
says. She has a streak of red paint across her forehead. "Let's stop for a while."

Nicole and my father go off to take a break.
They've been working on the room for two days
straight. They disappear behind the bedroom door
and leave me to get myself some lunch. Nicole
said I should help myself to whatever I find in her
fridge or cupboards. I eat a peanut butter sand-
wich, staring at the red tattoo parlour. A can of
black paint is sitting on a shelf, unopened. I want
to contribute my own touch to the room, but I
don't know if I should. I'm not the type of person
who does things without permission. But what the
heck? Do they expect me to just sit there all afternoon, twiddling my thumbs?

I tiptoe inside Tattoo Heaven. Standing in the
middle of the room is like standing in the middle
of a vat of blood. I feel like a small molecule in
the midst of the transfusion. I open the can of
black paint and grab a small brush. Then I dip the
tip into the paint and begin to stab black dots onto
the red paint around the door frame. I do the same
around the window frame. Out the window and
way to the left I can see the roof of the Verdun
Arena, and beside it, on either side, tall apartment

buildings that must back onto the river.

When I'm done, I stand back to check out my handiwork. I like it. I hope Nicole will, too. I think she will because her whole house is decorated with lots of wild patterns. I peeked into her bedroom earlier, on the way into Tattoo Heaven. It looked exotic, with Indian scarves hanging over her mirror and lampshades. The bed was covered in a wild tiger-striped bedspread, something my mother would never have in our house. And the walls were bright orange.

About an hour later my father and Nicole emerge looking sleepy, their clothes all rumpled. I wonder if they've really been napping, but I don't want to think about what else they could have been doing. I hold my breath as they head straight for the tattoo parlour.

"Jackie! What have you done?" I hear my father call out. He's standing right under the door frame, under the black spots. He sounds angry. I don't say anything.

"She's got your talent for colour, your little girl," Nicole says, laughing. She puts her finger over her lips, as if to shut my father up. "*Je l'aime.* I like it. Why not?"

Then she comes over to where I'm standing. "If only she'd let me repay her with a tattoo, a tulip or a mermaid. Something appropriate for a young girl about to spring into womanhood," she says, more to my father than to me.

I blush and almost die when she says this,

47

keeping my eyes on the black dots to avoid having to face either of them.

* * *

"And what wonderful thing did you do with your father today?" my mother asks when I get home, after I've handed her the envelope.

"Not much. We just hung out," I lie. I still haven't mentioned Nicole to my mother and she's never mentioned her to me, so I assume she still doesn't know. And even if she does ... I remember the happy expressions on my father's and Nicole's faces when they woke up from their nap and came out to look at their work in the shop. I can't exactly share that with my mother, can I?

"That sounds dull," she says. "The least he could do is take you out to a movie or something. You know, Jackie, you don't have to go with him if you don't want to. He can't force you. It's not like this is a legal arrangement or anything."

"It's okay," I say. "Forget it. It's not that bad." I look down at my nails. They're covered in black paint. When I lift my hand to brush the hair off my face I see another black spot on my elbow. But my mother doesn't seem to notice.

I could be spotted like a leopard at the moment and she probably wouldn't care. She must be thinking about Theresa. I have the feeling she can't wait for the weekend to be over and return her to Monday.

Then she can go back to her precious sick girl's house.

48

Chapter 7

"I've decided that today's the day, Jackie. I'm bringing you to Theresa's with me. I arranged it yesterday. You'll have to wear clean clothes and shower first. It's more important than ever to keep her environment really spotless. Wash your hands with that special disinfecting soap right before we leave. Okay?" My mother makes it sounds like I'm a walking ball of germs. If I'm such a threat, why take me over there? It's not like I want to go anyway.

"Finish eating and then go get ready," she adds, getting up herself.

"I don't want any more. I've lost my appetite," I say, throwing down my toast. I concentrate instead on drinking my tea, sweetened with three spoonfuls of sugar. I suddenly feel like gobbling down every sweet and sugary thing I can find to help take away the sour taste in my mouth. The last thing on earth I want to do is visit the sick girl.

"You can't go too close to her, keep your distance," my mother warns me on the way across the street. "And no touching. Mrs. Desjardins is very particular about that," she adds as she knocks on the door. Does she think I've been planning to throw my arms around the sick girl, like a long-lost buddy?

The sick girl's mother answers the door, beaming at us. This is obviously a momentous occasion. "Come in, come in! Welcome, Jackie. Theresa is down the hall, in her room. Come, I'll take you there." She says all this in the friendliest voice, thick as honey. Then she turns back to my mother and says, in a more serious voice, "Claire, our fridge is filthy. I'd like you to work on that today, okay?" We walk to the end of a long hallway on the first floor and stop outside a door that must be Theresa's. I turn back to see my mother hurry down the hall in the opposite direction, into what must be the kitchen, rolling up her sleeves, as if she can't wait to tackle the job.

"Theresa, you remember Jackie? She's come to play," the sick girl's mother announces. Come to play? People my age don't play. It's like these people are stuck in a time warp.

"Hi," I say. Theresa just nods, ever so slightly. She's dressed as I remember her, in a white blouse and pink skirt. The white knee socks her mother probably ordered her to wear are still rolled in a ball on her dresser. She is stretched out on her bed, leaning back against a mountain of white pillows.

She looks like she'd topple without them. I don't know where to go. Theresa's mother's already gone, probably to supervise my mother in the kitchen.

"Can I sit down?" I ask. Theresa gives me a "whatever" sort of shrug.

I sit gingerly on the edge of the bed because there are no chairs. I look around the room, trying to do it discreetly so Theresa won't notice. Definite time warp, I think. Posters of kittens and puppies, lots of stuffed animals, and even a couple of dolls on her bureau. The only thing that isn't childish is the Spice Girls poster from their movie, *Spice World*. It's at least five years old now, but it's the most up-to-date thing I can see.

"Did you see it, too?" Theresa asks suddenly. "You look like you've seen it, the way you're staring at the poster. I've seen it, about a dozen times. That's 'cause I own it. My mom bought it for me. I can't really go out to movies ever, so I watch a lot of videos. What about you? Do you like movies? Did you used to like the Spice Girls, too? I guess they're kind of passé now, right? I like Britney Spears, but my mother says she dresses like a slut. I don't think she dresses all that differently from the Spice Girls, if you asked me, but my mother doesn't really ask me much. She thinks she knows what's good for me. Does your mother act like a know-it-all, too? Mine does. She drives me crazy, but it's not like I can get away from her or anything. Sometimes I wish I could fly back

51

with my father when he goes back to the Gaspé, for his plane business, but my mother'd never let me. She'd say no, I just know it. Do you know what I mean?"

My mouth hangs open. I don't know which question to answer first. I don't know why, but I imagined that the sick girl wouldn't speak, as if I thought the chemotherapy would have zapped her vocal cords. But now I can see how wrong I was. She sure can speak. She can't get the words out fast enough. It's as though she's been saving her words for so long that now they're just flying out at me.

"If I could go to any concert I choose, I'd go see The Backstreet Boys. I like them, don't you? Not just 'cause they're cute, even though they are — well, some of them are. But I like their singing, their harmonies. I know something about harmony because I used to sing in a choir, The Gaspé Children's Choir, before I got sick. I was a soprano, which means I can sing high. Have you ever been in a choir? It's fun. We toured around a bit and won some competitions. I'm not in it anymore, but I keep in touch. The director sent me a CD that the choir cut last year. It was cool, but I'm not on it."

Then she stops talking and closes her eyes, as though the effort has drained her. Her skin is very pale, transparent almost. I don't know if I should say something about being sorry that she can't do all these things anymore. I don't know what to say to make her feel like she isn't missing out on anything. I feel like I should tell her that my life isn't just big, romping fun either.

"My father left home a while ago and has a new girlfriend," I blurt out after a moment of silence. I didn't plan to say this, but the words just flew out before I could stop them. Theresa doesn't respond. She just stares at me. I don't know if I should continue. Then she opens her mouth and points to her head.

"Do you think this is my real hair?" I shrug. My mother told me that Theresa now wears a wig, so I've been trying not to stare at her hair. "Well, it isn't. Do you think this is the colour of my real hair? Or do you think I chose a different colour just for fun, just to trick people?"

I am about to say something, but she bursts out again.

"Well, it is my real colour. Why would I want to pick a colour that wasn't my own? Then everyone would know it was fake. Is that what you think I want?"

Theresa is acting like I've accused her of something, when she was the one who brought up her hair in the first place. I feel completely helpless. I'm trying to think of something to say to explain myself, when suddenly Theresa's mother is standing at the door.

"You'd best be going now, Jackie. Theresa needs to rest. I hope you'll come back soon."

I turn to wave goodbye to the sick girl, but her

eyes are already closed. From the front porch I can see down the hall into the kitchen where my mother is on her hands and knees, her arms deep inside the fridge, scrubbing away. All the food has been emptied out onto the counters. I don't get a chance to call goodbye to her because Mrs. Desjardins ushers me out the door.

* * *

I haven't been able to get to sleep yet, even though it's past midnight. I can't stop thinking about the sick girl — Theresa. She seemed so different from the ghost-like girl who stood out on the deck every now and then. I keep seeing her talk. I don't hear the words. I just see her mouth open and moving, rambling on, as though she had millions of words locked up inside her, ready to release, like a huge bouquet of balloons finally cut free from their strings, floating up in a burst of colour to the sky.

I had thought that sitting so close to such illness would make me feel sick, but it didn't. It's like I was expecting her wounds to be on the outside, to show somehow. Instead, she looks like any other fourteen-year-old girl, except for the fake hair and pale skin. She could almost be one of those young supermodels, the ones that look anorexic, with their hip bones sticking out of the tops of their jeans, like Kate Moss.

Theresa's definitely not what I expected.

Chapter 8

That Sunday I actually see Nicole giving someone a tattoo for the very first time. It's her cousin, Josée, who's in visiting from Quebec City. Nicole says it's a family ritual, tattooing relatives she hasn't seen in a while. Nicole didn't actually invite me into her tattoo parlour, but she did leave the door to the kitchen open, so I just kind of wander in. My father had to leave to finish a rush job and is only expected back later. It's the first time I've been alone with Nicole, so I'm kind of glad that Josée has shown up.

I curl up in a ball in the corner of the shop and just watch and listen. This cousin doesn't speak much English. My French is pretty good because I'm in French immersion at school, but these two speak it at the speed of light. I can only pick out the odd word or phrase. Josée likes to add, *c'est pas possible?* and *ça se peux-tu?* to the ends of her sentences. Then they both crack up.

Josée has asked for an anchor above her ankle, because her boyfriend is in the navy and is away now in the Persian Gulf. From what I can make out of the conversation, she wants the anchor to keep her *pieds à terre*, or her feet on the ground, while he's gone. They seem to understand this as a code phrase for something else because they keep laughing and talking about all the guys they've both gone out with. I wonder if they'd be having this conversation if my father were around.

Nicole puts on her rubber gloves and removes a needle from inside a steel machine. Some steam escapes the lid when she lifts it. She attaches the needle to a long electrical cord. It looks kind of like a dentist's drill. When the first needle sinks in, drawing blood, I cover my face with my hands. Josée, who already has three other tattoos that I can see, doesn't flinch.

Nicole's back sort of covers most of the operation, so I amuse myself by studying the stencils in the binders on her shelves and imagining what kind of tattoo I would get if I ever changed my mind. Would I actually have the nerve to get something daring, like a giant dragon? And what would people say when they see me back at school for the start of Grade 9? They'd think I flipped. I'm not known as a colourful girl. I'm the kind of girl who just sort of blends in — no loud jewellery, no purple streaks in my hair, no body piercing. Just kind of plain. The only thing that made me stand out last year was the fact that Alex became my boyfriend in April.

When they're done, Nicole looks straight at me and says, "So, little girl, do you like it?" I didn't realize she even knew I was here. "Does it make you want one now?" She and Josée laugh.

"Not really," I say. "It looks painful."

"Ç'est pas mal. It's not so bad," says Josée. Then Nicole grabs a bottle of wine from the table behind her and she and Josée disappear into the living room. I follow them and sit in the rocking chair across from the sofa they're stretched out on, one at either end. I feel like I'm intruding, but I'm kind of stuck here until my father comes back. He was supposed to be here an hour ago. I don't know why he bothered picking me up today if he knew he'd be away all afternoon.

Nicole and Josée talk non-stop. I've never seen two grown-ups who have so much to talk about. They're tripping over each other at times to get a word in. I wonder if I could ever chatter happily like that as an adult. People are always telling me I'm too quiet, especially Katie.

Every now and then Nicole looks at me and winks, to let me know she's aware I'm here. She pushes a bowl of chips in my direction with her toes, nodding her chin as though to give me permission to take some, but then Josée keeps pulling the bowl back. She eats chips faster than she talks.

What seems like hours later, my father returns. I'm curled up in the rocking chair, half asleep. My stomach is gurgling with hunger. No one fed me, well, apart from the chips. It's way past my usual suppertime. It's also past the time my father was supposed to take me home.

Nicole jumps up when my father comes in, grabs his hand and leads him over to Josée, who stands up and kisses my father on both cheeks. Then she looks at Nicole and laughs, nodding her head as though she's agreeing to something.

"*Il est cute, non?*" Nicole says. Cute? My father is cute? Josée must agree because she is smiling.

"What've you ladies been up to?" my father asks as Nicole hands him a glass of wine. Nicole tugs up the hem of Josée's jeans, exposing the bandage.

"Ah, of course." It's only as my father is sitting down on the sofa between them that he looks across the room and notices me.

"Jackie!" he exclaims. It's like he is accusing me of suddenly materializing out of nowhere. I can feel myself turn red.

"Oh, *mon Dieu!*" Nicole says. "She is still here, your little girl." Then she laughs. I don't see what's so funny. Where did she think I'd gone? "She is too quiet. She is like a mouse."

I don't say anything. What is there to say? I couldn't exactly join in their conversation, could I? Was I supposed to start telling my father's girl-friend about my love life? As if I have one now that Alex is gone.

"Her mother's going to shoot me," my father says. He puts his wine glass down with a sigh, as though it's something he really regrets having to do. "Come on, I'd better get you home." I can hear Nicole and Josée chuckling the whole time we're leaving. My father barely says a word to me in the car. When we pull up outside the house, he says, "Have a good week, okay?" Then he hands me the weekly wad of cash as I'm opening the car door.

My stomach lets out a huge growl in response.

Chapter 9

On Wednesday my mother asks me to come back to Theresa's. "Your visit really helped cheer her up last time," she says.

"I don't know why. I barely said ten words to her," I say. I also can't see what we'll ever find in common to talk about if Theresa likes The Backstreet Boys. I wonder if she even knows they no longer exist. I think they've each been sucked up into other crappy boy bands — one of them was even exposed as a drug addict. And I wish Theresa at least had a chair so I wouldn't have to practically sit on top of her.

To my surprise, when I get to her room today, a white chair has been placed by the side of her bed. Maybe Theresa didn't like me sitting on top of her, either. Like last time, she barely acknowledges my presence. Then, all of a sudden, as if a light switch has been flicked on, she turns to me and starts talking.

"I wanted to ask you last time but I didn't get a chance whether or not you have a boyfriend. You look like the kind of girl who has a boyfriend, 'cause you're pretty. I mean, not that all pretty girls have boyfriends. I guess some of the big stars don't even have boyfriends. You'd never expect gorgeous girls who look like them to be single. There should be guys lined up around the block waiting for the chance to go out with them. In fact, maybe there are but they just don't really like any of them. It would be hard to tell if someone really liked you for yourself if you were that famous or whether they just liked you because of how famous you are. And they could want your money, too. You never know."

The whole time Theresa is talking I'm trying to remember her original question, about whether I have a boyfriend. I guess I should tell her about Alex. I think he's still my boyfriend, even though I haven't heard from him in a while. He said he'd call me when he came back to Montreal, but so far I haven't heard from him. Should I tell Theresa all these things? But before I can even think how to phrase my answer, she starts talking again.

"I hope you don't mind me asking about your personal life. My mother says I'm too curious, that it isn't good for me. She says I just have to be patient and when I'm better I can get out there and find things out for myself. Not that I have anyone to ask things around here, but I watch a lot of TV to try to keep up with what's going on. I like the entertainment news the best. The real news is depressing, don't you think? It's all about war and terrorism and stuff. But I like finding out what's up with the stars."

Should I tell her about Alex now? Theresa's cheeks have turned pink, probably from the exertion of talking so fast.

"Well, I do have a…"

"I knew it!" she jumps in. "There was something about you. It seemed like you've had some experience. I can usually tell. When I meet other kids at the hospital, that's how I amuse myself. I try to figure out how much experience they had, before they got sick. You just sort of carry yourself like someone who's had a boyfriend. I don't. I'm sure you can tell. It's not like I could go out with anyone anyway. I'm so stuck in here. The only guys I meet are sick like me. Some of them are cute, at least they are before they lose their hair. Some of them look okay without hair, too. You wouldn't believe how flirtatious sick guys can be. I guess that's guys, right? Nothing stops them. Even during chemo, with needles stuck up their arms, they can still be hitting on you, I swear. I bet you don't believe me."

Now my mouth is hanging open to my knees. I have absolutely no idea what to say.

"Sure. I mean, my boyfriend Alex is always trying to get me…"

"I could tell that, too. I mean, that makes sense, right? You're his girlfriend and you're pretty, like

I said." Then, as if the last kernel of energy has been expelled from Theresa's thin body, her head flops to the side and she closes her eyes. I wonder what I should do. Should I just sit here and see if she wakes up again or should I leave? I wonder, too, how much more I would have told her if she hadn't turned off like that. Was I really going to tell her that Alex was trying to have sex with me? I barely know this girl and already I'm telling her more than Katie knows. Katie thinks Alex is some kind of god. She's always telling me how lucky I am 'cause he's so cute and so sweet. She says any guy who can take such care putting delicate tooth-pick bridges together has to be really careful about other people's feelings, so I'm in good hands. Whenever I even think about telling her some of what he does or says to me I stop myself. I'm afraid she'll be angry because she pretty much got us together in the first place. She's the one who pushed me into the seat beside him on the band bus. And she's the one who had already planted the seed in Alex's head by telling him that I had a massive crush on him. Which wasn't really true. It was more like she thought I should have one. So we're together because of Katie in the first place.

And why does Theresa keep going on about how pretty I am? I'm not pretty at all compared to someone like Nicole. She's pretty. In fact, she's gorgeous. I'll never be as gorgeous as her, not if I try for the rest of my life.

It's strange, but talking to Theresa has left me

feeling deflated somehow. I'm like a balloon with a teeny hole in it that has been seeping air slowly. She looks pretty empty herself. I watch her sleep and think about how the veins in her forehead show through her light skin.

I tiptoe out of the room and close the door softly behind me.

Chapter 10

"She is quiet today, your little girl, quieter than usual," Nicole says to my father. We're sitting in Nicole's living room, not doing much. We've been here for two hours and I've barely said a word. My father just shrugs. It isn't the type of thing he'd notice. Besides, he's watching a baseball game on TV. He never apologized for forgetting about me last week. I almost didn't come with him today, just to pay him back. But I couldn't really think of an excuse, so here I am. Plus, I kind of look forward to my Sundays at Nicole's. I like watching her. I find myself trying to take notes on how she moves and how she talks. Everything she does just thrills my father so much, there must be something about her that's textbook stuff. I might need to refer back to these notes when I see Alex this week. He called to say he's coming home for a couple of days. I figure I might as well try to get back in his good books. It would be nice to be in someone's good books right about now. If I could just learn how to mimic the way Nicole throws her head back and laughs when my father pecks her neck, instead of getting embarrassed, I might do okay with Alex.

"Are you coming to help me in the kitchen?" Nicole asks my father, who's now flipping channels since his baseball game is finished. "I'm going to start dinner."

"Sure," he responds. My mother would be floored. I don't think my father knows where we keep the pots in our kitchen.

"And you, little girl, do you want to help, too?"

"No, it's okay. I'll stay here."

"*C'est ton choix*. It's your choice," Nicole says, taking my father's hand.

I stretch out on the jungle-patterned sofa and watch music videos with the mute button on. I find them more amusing this way. People look really stupid dancing without music. As a bunch of half-naked girls dance on top of an airplane wing, I find myself thinking about Theresa. I see her lying thin as a wisp on her bed, her fake hair like a bunch of straw on the mountain of pillows. I keep going over her words again and again, and all I can tease out of them is her easy acceptance of her condition. She doesn't seem bothered by the fact that she can't go to movies or to concerts or that she can't sing anymore. Or by the fact that she can't go out and meet guys. She seems resigned to it all. I wonder if I'm too resigned to all the changes in my life — my parents are sepa-rated, my mother's obsessed with Theresa and her illness, my father is in love and acting like a teenager with his new girlfriend, who wants to tat-too me. I haven't really fought at all against any of these changes. Should I have? Should I have tried to stop my father from leaving? Should I have tried to make my mother do something to win him back, although I can't imagine what that would be?

I've just been sitting back, watching it all hap-pen, as though my parents are part of a made-for-TV movie, one with a sucky title, like *Back to His Teens* or *Cleaning for a Cause*. Come to think of it, the movie couple wouldn't even have a daughter. There'd be nowhere to fit her into the story. Just like in real life. I don't really fit into this script, either. At home, my mother uses me to unload about Theresa and the latest developments in her illness. At Nicole's, they put up with me, but nothing they do depends on my being here. Even now, I can hear chopping and laughing, the vegetables sizzling in hot oil, and the corks being yanked out of bottles of wine.

There isn't one thing that would be happening differently without me. It reminds me of the way Theresa's choir produced the CD without her. The loss of her voice probably didn't leave any holes. The other voices filled the gap, the way sand rushes in to fill in holes scooped out at the beach.

Even Alex doesn't seem to be missing me.

When he called, he said he has a whole new gang of friends to hang out with in his father's town. I waited for him to say he missed me, but he never did. I got the feeling that the new group of friends included a new girlfriend. Probably one who doesn't mind having her bra yanked out from under her T-shirt. She might even take it off herself, saving Alex the trouble.

"Come and eat, mademoiselle," Nicole calls out. I enter the kitchen and discover that Nicole has covered the table with a white tablecloth and set it with fancy, flowered dishes. Two tall, silver candelabrum stand in the centre. Nicole bends down to light the red candles, holding back her long hair so it won't trail in the flame. I bet her hair would even go on fire elegantly, the flames spiralling up in a graceful pattern. Tall, delicate wine glasses sit in front of each plate. Nicole fills mine with a tiny amount of wine, winking at me as she pours. "She's allowed, *non*, your little girl?"

"Of course," my father replies, his eyes on Nicole.

"Well, what do you think?" Nicole asks when I take a bite of the fancy chicken, which is covered with a creamy pink sauce.

"It's good!" I say. I've never tasted anything like it. I'm beginning to think there's nothing Nicole can't do well. No wonder my father has fallen in love with her. It would be hard not to. My mother only makes chicken one way. I picture her shaking the chicken in the plastic bag, turning it so that the batter clings evenly to the pieces of meat. When I was really young, she'd cut the chicken into bite-sized balls before coating them, so that I could just pop them into my mouth with my fingers. With each bite I take of Nicole's gourmet chicken, I feel I'm erasing my mother and the years of batter-coated chicken that she set on plates before us. I feel incredibly guilty for enjoying myself so much.

Then my father raises his glass. "A toast to us," he says, clinking the side of Nicole's glass. I don't know if I should hold mine up. Who is "us"? Does he mean all three of us, or just him and Nicole? It never even occurs to me that us could mean me and him. But then he raises his glass toward me, so I lift mine and we clink, too.

"Tell your little girl what we're celebrating," Nicole says.

"It's our anniversary," my father declares, beaming.

I think I'm going to be sick. Isn't this a bit over the top? How can you have an anniversary when you've only been together a few weeks? Then Nicole backs up her chair and goes to the cupboard over the sink, where she pulls out a wrapped box. "*Pour toi,*" she says, handing it to my father. Then he pulls something out of his shirt pocket, a smaller wrapped box. My heart stops. What if it's an engagement ring? Is it even legal to get engaged when you're still married? And could Nicole really become my stepmother? What if they have kids? Any kids of Nicole's would be gorgeous, even with my father's genes to spoil the mix.

They open their gifts together, both of them grinning like kids on Christmas morning. Nicole has bought my father a pocket watch on a chain. He keeps flipping the lid up and laughing, as though he's never seen anything as amazing. I'm relieved to see that my father's gift to Nicole is a locket in the shape of a raindrop. Inside, he's placed a tiny picture of himself. Nicole seems to love it. She puts it around her neck and opens it every few seconds, as if she can't remember whose face is in it. Then they reach across the table and kiss, two inches away from the flame.

I want to crawl under the table. I feel like I've intruded on a private moment. If I weren't here, they'd be wrapped in each other's arms. When my father flips open his new watch, I imagine he's counting the hours until he can finally take me home.

Nicole refills their wine glasses and holds her glass up high. "We've known each other six months today," she says, leaning toward my father until her head is almost on his shoulder. My father shoots me a quick glance and then looks down. His entire face and even his bald spot are turning a deep pink.

"Oops," Nicole says, covering her mouth with her napkin. "Maybe I shouldn't have said that in front of your little girl, eh?" My father doesn't say anything. He just puts his hand over Nicole's, as though she's the one who needs reassuring.

I put down my fork and count the months backward on my fingers under the table. That means they met in February, in the winter. I slam my knife and fork onto my plate and glare at my father. He's still staring at his plate.

"It's better you know, *non*? No more secrets," Nicole says.

"And what about my mother, does she know?" I ask, glaring at the two of them. They each have a thin mustache of red wine on their upper lips. I wish I could slap them away.

"Jackie!" my father says angrily, finally looking up. "What your mother knows has nothing to do with you."

"No, you're right. It has nothing to do with me. Nothing has anything to do with me," I snap back. This meal certainly had nothing to do with me. Why did they have to do this now? Wouldn't it have been better without me?

My mind flies back to Theresa, lying all alone in her room, totally cut off. Is this how she feels all the time, like she's completely outside of everything? Is this how she felt even four years ago at my party, watching me and my friends chatter and giggle?

"Take me home, please," I say to my father.

"Jackie. Just finish your chicken. It's all done now. Nothing can be changed." Is he talking about the chicken or my life?

"I just want to go home," I say again, very quietly and slowly. I need to stay in control here. I need to get him to take me home.

71

"Take her if she wants," says Nicole. "She needs some time."

I look at Nicole. I can't believe that an hour ago I was admiring her, trying to study her moves so that I could become more like her. Right now, I'd just like to dump the pink creamy sauce into her blond hair.

In the car, I think about how when my father showed me his Model-T tattoo, I assumed he had just gotten it. But it must have been there for months, hidden under his sleeve.

He was just waiting for the right time to roll it out of the garage.

Chapter 11

I'm hanging out at Alex's this afternoon. He's letting his hair grow and can almost pull it into a ponytail. There's stubble all over his chin and upper lip. I can't decide if I like it or not. He's obviously trying to look like a grungy rock star. I guess he's switching from rap to rock.

I've only been here ten minutes when his mother calls upstairs to say that she's going out for a while. The minute he hears the garage door close, Alex pulls me onto the bed beside him. "Alone at last," he says, trying to kiss me. The whiskers on his face are really sharp and his chin feels like sandpaper next to mine. I twist away from him, but he persists. After a few minutes he leans back, annoyed.

"What's your problem?" he snaps.

The anger in his voice makes me hold still and Alex is finally able to catch hold of me long enough to really get into the kiss. His tongue is pushing my mouth open and his hand is starting to wander under my top. I can feel the room getting awfully hot all of a sudden. Alex is leaning over me now. His long brown hair is falling into my face.

"How's the carpentry business going?" I ask when he pulls back an inch to catch his breath, hoping I can ignite a conversation that will make him back off. We've been going out together for four months and I know he thinks it's time we did it. He's never said it in so many words, but he doesn't have to. It's usually written all over his face. The thing with Alex is that he's used to winning. He wins every competition he enters.

"Hey, that's work. I don't want to talk about work right now. Do you?"

No, I guess I don't really care about his dad's carpentry business. I'm just trying to find something to talk about. I don't suppose he'd want to hear about my father and Nicole, about how I now know they were actually seeing each other while my father was still living at home. I guess that explains him sleeping on the couch. It might also explain my mother's behaviour through the spring, the way she seemed to always be sitting at the kitchen table, staring into cups of tea long after they'd gone cold, her buttons done up wrong on her old housecoat so she looked lopsided. But if she knows about Nicole, why hasn't she ever asked about her?

"Didn't you miss me?" Alex asks, biting my lip.

"Oh, sure," I say.

"Well then?" My T-shirt flies across the room and lands on Alex's computer screen. It's as though he planned the shot, so that the big square eye couldn't watch us. Now, he's pulling my bra straps down. He can't unhook it 'cause it's a sports bra, the one-piece kind. I didn't wear it on purpose, but now I'm glad I did. I've never been naked in front of a guy before, not even Alex. The only other time we came this close was on my backyard swing, in the dark.

Alex is pushing down hard on me now with his whole body. My bra is down around my waist. My breasts look incredibly white, like poached eggs. They feel tingly where Alex has been squeezing them. A spot on my neck is stinging where Alex has been sucking it. It's funny, but when I see scenes like this in movies I put myself in the girl's place and they make me feel all warm inside. But now that I'm in the girl's place, it's all happening way too fast.

"We should do this before I disappear back to Ontario for the summer," Alex whispers in my ear. I don't say yes and I don't say no. I know that, either way, I'll regret my decision. Alex is starting to pull down the zipper on my jeans. I suddenly feel like one of his delicate toothpick bridges, so delicate I might break.

I take a deep breath and close my eyes and decide that whatever happens, I'll just let it happen. I can't seem to stop it anyway. At least Alex is interested in me. Right now, he's completely focused on me and nobody else. Isn't that what I wanted? An activity that I'm at the centre of? Something that depends on my being there. Alex couldn't be doing this alone, could he?

I also imagine what Katie would say if she knew that I had the chance to lose my virginity with a hot guy like Alex and didn't. Not only what Katie would say, but what any of the girls at school would say. They think Alex looks like Johnny Depp 'cause he has the same sort of cute smile and dark eyes.

My jeans are sliding over my hips, exposing my yellow underpants with the word Monday on them, when the phone rings. Alex ignores it, but whoever is calling isn't giving up. "Shit," Alex says, finally getting up. His own jeans are down around his ankles and he almost trips leaping across his room. I pull his abandoned shirt over me to cover up. Alex is sitting with his back to me, hunched over his desk. He's talking low, like he might not want me to hear. I hear him say, "Nothing, not much." That means whoever's on the other end has just asked what he's doing. Then I hear him say, "I can't right now, I'll call you back later."

"Who was it?" I ask when he saunters back over to the bed, his pants back in place, his face all red.

"Just a friend from Lancaster," he says. "No one special." Alex doesn't look directly at me when he says this. His eyes have that same down-cast look that my father's had yesterday when Nicole mentioned that they had been together for six months.

"Now, where were we?" he says, starting to lean back over me. I'm trying to sit up. I have a really sick feeling in my stomach, like I'm being smothered. I'm working up the nerve to tell Alex that I don't believe him, that I know he must have been talking to a girl, when his bedroom door bangs open. His little brother comes thumping into the room, screaming that he's going to tell his mother. Then he grabs my T-shirt off the computer and runs away with it.

While Alex chases his brother around the house, I take the opportunity to put myself back together.

I grab one of his shirts from the pile of clothes on his bed and leave by the back door. Alex's voice is shouting "I'm going to kill you!" in the background. Even though he's probably yelling at his brother, I feel his words directed at me, each one hitting me like a stone.

Chapter 12

My mother's surprised when I meet her at the
front door the next morning just as she is about to
set off for Theresa's.

"Can I come?" I ask. My mother hesitates,
looking down at me like she can't believe she
heard right. I kind of can't believe it myself. I just
don't want to stay home alone today. If I do, I'll
go crazy. I thought I had enough to think about
with Nicole, but now the thing with Alex yesterday is haunting me.

"Jackie, that would be so nice." My mother
puts down her pail of supplies, gently puts her
arms around me, and pulls me close to her. I can't
remember being pressed up against her like this
since I was ten. I like it. I feel my body relax as I
breathe in her pre-workday scent of deodorant and
soap. We seem to stand like that for the longest
time, until she pulls back. "I'm sure Theresa will
appreciate it, Jackie, but I should just pop over

and tell her mother first, okay? She may want Theresa to change out of her pajamas and freshen up. I'll call you from there."

I stand on the porch and watch my mother cross the street. She has to wait for a car to pass first, then she does a little hop before taking off. It suddenly occurs to me that my mother is looking really good. I hadn't noticed that before today. The change happened so slowly, yet so definitely. She seems to have lost weight, and there's a spring in her step that hasn't been there for ages. If my mother knew about Nicole all along, that could be why she let herself go so badly. Some days, I'd come home from school to find her still in the old sweatsuit she'd gone to sleep in, her hair obviously unbrushed and her breath stale from yesterday's food. When I found my father doing his own laundry I blamed my mother. I thought it was her fault for growing ugly and lazy and never moving off the kitchen chair, drinking buckets of tea that were staining her teeth a deep brownish yellow.

She sure doesn't look like that anymore. She looks the way she did when I was little, her hair cut short and perky around her face, her blue eyes sparkling. And she's smiling more than she has in ages.

The phone rings, jerking me back to the present. My mother tells me that Theresa and her mother are delighted that I want to visit and to come right over.

When I'm settled on the chair beside Theresa's bed, she pulls herself upright. She's still in a rumpled, beige nightgown that she obviously slept in. I wonder if she only dressed up the first two times I visited because I was new to her then. Maybe now she can just be herself and not try to hide her illness, or camouflage it with preppy clothes. As if Theresa can tell what I'm thinking, she starts straightening her nightclothes, and then she just bursts out talking.

"Sorry I'm not dressed, but I didn't know I'd need to get dressed today. I didn't know I was going to be doing anything. I only get dressed when I have to go to the hospital for treatments or to see my doctor. They've taken enough blood from me to pump Frankenstein's monster up. I've been reading that book. Have you ever read it? It's pretty amazing, especially when you think that Mary Shelley was only nineteen when she wrote it. Can you imagine writing a book like that five years from now and then that book gets to be so famous Hollywood turns it into a dozen films, and hundreds of years later people are still reading it? That would be amazing. I could use all my experiences at the hospital to write a book about a monster put together with body parts, believe me. Some of the kids I've shared rooms with have lost body parts already. Sure, sometimes they get new ones from donors, but that's pretty much what the monster in Frankenstein is made from, except his donors were actually dead bodies, which, if you think about it, would be really good if we could do that. I've known a few kids at the hospital who died waiting for kidneys or livers or, once, even a heart."

Once again, I don't know what to say. I have absolutely no experience with illness beyond flu and colds and one broken toe that got run over by some idiot's skateboard at school.

Theresa's curtains are drawn and her window must be closed because the room is stuffy. I wonder if she notices.

"Do you mind if I open your curtains and window? It's really nice out."

Theresa just shrugs. Then she starts up again. "Did you know that long ago they kept sick people in totally sealed rooms 'cause they thought the fresh air would hurt them 'cause it might be full of germs? That's not why my room's all closed up, but I just like to think about things like that. Like back in the middle ages during the black plague they would open up the sewers to let the germs go down the hole, which of course isn't what happened. Just the opposite. The rats came up and spread more plague germs around the city. I guess you can tell I watch a lot of Discovery Television. I'm supposed to be keeping up with schoolwork through correspondence, but it's hard, so my mother lets me watch as much "good" television as I want. When she's not around I can switch over to MuchMusic."

It sounds like the only things Theresa's connected to are other sick kids, television, her mother, and this vague correspondence school. I suddenly have an idea.

"Hey, Theresa," I cut in, maybe a little too loudly

because she looks startled. "Do you want to come outside with me? It'd be fun."

Theresa's eyes grow really large in their sockets. I take that as a sign of encouragement. "Let's find you some clothes, okay? Where do you keep them?" I see some sweatpants hanging off a hook behind her door. Those'll do. She certainly doesn't need to put on the party gear she usually wears to stand outside. I throw her the pants and a T-shirt that I found under them. "Get dressed," I say, trying to sound forceful. I turn around to give her some privacy. I'm not sure if she's doing what I asked, but I do hear the rustling sounds of material being manipulated, slowly.

"Ready?" I ask.

"I guess," she replies. She sounds hesitant.

"Okay, let's go," I say. But when I turn around I see that she hasn't moved from her spot on the bed. At least she is dressed, though. "Come on, Theresa. Don't you want to?" She nods and begins to stir. Her movements are slow and deliberate, as though each change of position is a challenge.

"Here, I'll help you." I take her legs and swing them gently over the side of her bed and then put my hands under her arms to pull her up. Once she's upright, I hook my right arm into her left and we walk out of the room.

I can feel the slackness of her arm muscle under mine, as though it's made of cotton candy. This may be harder than I thought.

I hope I know what the hell I'm doing.

Chapter 13

We don't bump into anyone the whole way down the hall and out the front door, which isn't what I expected. I thought we'd see our mothers, but they're obviously off doing stuff elsewhere, probably upstairs. I can't decide if I should leave Theresa and go find someone to ask for permission first. It's not like I'm doing anything terrible. We'll probably just sit on her deck. Theresa sure looks like she could use some sun. Besides, she would have said something herself if she needed to ask first, wouldn't she? She knows her own mother better than I do.

The mid-morning sun is really bright on Theresa's stone deck. I help her lean against the railing. "I'll just go find us some chairs," I say. I saw some folding ones piled against the house earlier on. I take two up to the deck, unfold them, and then help Theresa into hers. I have pointed the chairs to face the hot rays.

Theresa looks completely happy. Her eyes are closed and her face is pointed up at the sun as though she is trying to hook every bit of its warmth with her bony chin. Her mouth looks like it's smiling and for once she is completely quiet. Another idea comes to me.

"Hey, when's the last time you took a walk around the neighbourhood, Theresa?" I don't see why we should limit ourselves to this square porch.

"My mother doesn't let me go further than this," Theresa replies. I think I detect a sad note in her voice.

"Would you want to do it, though?"

"Sure, I guess. I mean, I'd like to see something different … I guess."

"Okay then, let's do it," I say. "We'll just walk to the corner and back. I'm sure you'll be all right." I stand over Theresa and hold out my hand. She places her tiny hand in mine. It's as light and white as a piece of tissue.

We take the front steps slowly, then turn right and start up the street. This isn't the most exciting street in the world. There are only six houses between us and the corner, and most of them look the same: two-storey, brown brick houses with sloping roofs that extend over the garage. People have tried to individualize them by putting up awnings or second-floor balconies from the master bedrooms. One has turned the top of the garage into a terrace, another into a whole solarium. I wonder if Theresa notices these differences. We stop at the foot of each walkway and she looks up at the house and stares at it intently as though she's making a deep mental picture to draw on later. I guess anything's exciting if all you've seen is the inside of your bedroom for the last four years, apart from hospitals. As we're walking, I tell Theresa the names of all the people who live in the houses that we're passing, or as much as I can tell her. It's not like I know everyone that well.

"Tell me about their pets," Theresa says.

"Pets? Umm, I'm not sure if I can. I do know that the people over there, the Milmines, have a golden retriever named Max. He's a really friendly dog. Mr. Singh has three cats. They like to pee in our yard."

"Do you have pets?" asks Theresa.

"I used to have a cat named Igor, but he vanished a couple of months ago. I put up some signs, but we never found him." Poor Igor. He disappeared at a bad time. I was the only person who seemed to care.

"That's the first thing I'm going to get when I'm better," Theresa says. "A cat or a dog. My mother freaks out when anything with fur comes near me. My dad brought back a puppy from the Gaspé once. It was one of my cousin's dog's newborns. It was a chocolate lab, absolutely adorable." Theresa stops walking whenever she talks, as though she can't do both at once.

"What happened?"

"My mother wouldn't let me keep it, because of

the fur and germs. And she said nobody would be able to walk it. My father's away too much, and she's too busy with me."

"Oh, that's too bad," I say. I try to think of something to change the subject. "If we just keep going one more block, then turn the corner for another short block, we'd hit Alex's house."

"Who's Alex?"

"He is, or *was*, my boyfriend. I'm not even sure he's still speaking to me." I wonder what Alex would say if I showed up at his door with Theresa. I picture him taking in Theresa's bony body, which actually looks like it could be made of toothpicks. He wouldn't have a clue what to say to her.

"Or, if we went that way," I say, pointing diagonally to the right, "I could show you Katie's house. She's my best friend. But she's not here, either. She's away in Nova Scotia." I realize I've just shown Theresa the whole triangle of my world: from my house to Alex's to Katie's.

"Look at that," Theresa gasps suddenly, pointing at a hedge beside the last house. "Isn't it pretty?" I'm not sure what she's looking at.

"You mean that?" I point to a long orange caterpillar that's inching its way up a branch, accordion style.

"Can I touch it?"

"I guess so." I wonder if Theresa's mother would count this as fur.

Theresa runs her tiny finger along the creature's body, stopping it dead in its tracks. She does it over and over, stroking the caterpillar as though it's a persian cat. Each time, the caterpillar contracts until it eventually turns into a tight nugget of fur and falls off the branch altogether. Theresa is completely enchanted. "That was so cool," she says. "My mother would never let me do that." I'm glad she's so happy. I've never seen her this excited before.

We swivel at the corner to head back. Maybe I can turn this walk into some kind of game, where I quiz Theresa on the houses and their inhabitants and pets on the way back. But then something happens. We're approaching the driveway of the second house when Theresa just stops dead and hangs her head down.

Her body, which was so feather-light up to now, seems to grow heavy as she leans against me.

"I can't," she says. "I'm so thirsty."

I'm thirsty, too. I was hoping that, for some lucky reason, Theresa wouldn't be. Maybe I thought a thin body like hers wouldn't need much water. I move her as best I can into a spot of shade cast by a large maple tree.

"We're almost back at your place, Theresa. Just hang in there, okay?" I try to move her with my leg. She's stiff as wood, but eventually she starts walking. I keep her on the inside, close to the hedges, where there is at least some occasional shade. I see a garden hose coiled carelessly on a front lawn and think about getting her a drink somehow, but I can't let go or she'll crumple.

Her mother will kill me when we get back. And what will mine say? She'll regret hugging me this morning and being so moved by my desire to brighten up Theresa's day.

I don't know how, but we manage to struggle back up onto Theresa's deck. Her face is as red as a tomato. There's no way her mother won't notice that we've been out in the sun for the last hour. I have a horrible image of her skin blistering overnight and then peeling off in thin layers, like a red onion's. And what if I've completely dehydrated her and made her illness worse? What if that's the reason she's never outside and why her curtains were drawn — to keep her out of the harmful sun? And what if she's picked up some weird caterpillar germ that can attack her weak immune system?

We enter the house, still undetected. I help Theresa up on her bed then hurry out to fetch some water. Unfortunately, I run smack into Theresa's mother in the hallway.

"Oh, you're still here, Jackie. You mustn't tire Theresa out. She needs all her strength for the next round of treatments."

"Oh, I was just leaving, Mrs. Desjardins. I'm getting some water then I'll go say goodbye."

"Okay, then." Theresa's mother disappears up the stairs. I assume that my mother is up there, too.

I take the full glass of water into Theresa's room. Her head is collapsed onto the pillow, her cheeks are still blood red, her eyes closed. I can't tell if she's asleep or passed out.

"Theresa, here, drink this," I say right beside her ear. She opens her eyes. I hold the glass to her lips and help her drink. She finishes it all, taking the tiniest of sips. Then she closes her eyes again.

What else can I do? I simply leave, depositing the empty glass in the sink on my way out.

It's only when I'm back home that I realize Theresa's mother will probably notice that her daughter is now dressed.

Anyway, it's done now and I can't undo it. In my mind, I see Theresa stroking the fluffy caterpillar. She looked so happy.

That can't be a bad thing, can it?

Chapter 14

"A bone marrow transplant is a very finicky treat-
ment. The donor can't just be anybody. They have
to be a perfect match. Theresa has no brothers or sis-
ters. She's an only child, like you. That makes the
chances of them finding the perfect match even
slimmer. Mrs. Desjardins told me that even with sib-
lings, only one in four might be suitable. God, when
you think of it, you'd always have to have five kids
just to make sure they'd all be safe for something
like this. But who can predict? And then there's
cousins and such, but they all live miles away. Her
mother is frantic already, even though everyone is
praying that it doesn't ever come down to it."

Theresa's mother isn't the only frantic one
around. My mother is sitting at the kitchen table
across from me, biting her nails the whole time
she's telling me this sad story. I keep waiting for
her to grill me on what I did with Theresa when
I visited her two days ago. Surely if Theresa had

a vicious sunburn it would show.

"Mom. Last time I saw Theresa she was looking a little ... uh ... red. Was she still red today?"

"Red? Good heavens, no! The poor thing is as pale as ever."

That explains why my mother hasn't gone berserk about the condition of Theresa's skin. I guess her face was red more from exertion than sun after all, and now her skin has settled back to its usual white hue, with just a touch of pink. Maybe the sun actually did her some good, although all this talk about bone marrow transplants makes that hope seem silly.

"Her mother will be tested, of course, and her father, but parents don't usually match. You'd think they would. I mean, who could be closer genetically? But it's the mixture, you see. You get so much from your mother and so much from your father and it all mixes up, like a stew, I suppose. If neither of them matches, or the cousins they can persuade, they'll start going outside on the off chance, if they need to."

I wonder what would happen if I offered to get tested. What if for some fluky biological reason, Theresa and I were a perfect bone marrow match? Then the doctors could extract the good stuff from me and inject it into Theresa's body to help her get well. Part of me would always be there, inside Theresa's body, keeping her white and red blood cells in check. It would almost be like having a sister, a blood sister.

"And of course I'm going to get tested, too. I have to. I can't just stand by and not do it."

My mother's words hit me like a slap in the face. She's going to do it. Why her? Isn't this above and beyond the call of duty for a house-keeper? I've gotten used to the idea of her sucking up Theresa's dust and ridding her toilet of germs, especially now that I've gotten to know Theresa. But that doesn't mean I want my mother to give Theresa her bone marrow.

If she and Theresa are a perfect match, a part of my mother will always be inside of Theresa, help-ing her live. They'll be more connected than me and my mother. In some ways, I think they already are. Come to think of it, the only reason she hugged me the other day was because I wanted to do something for Theresa. I can't believe I've actually been feeling sorry for my mother. I've been working so hard at keeping Nicole a secret, being deliberately vague whenever my mother asks what my father and I have done. I didn't want her to feel jealous, or left out. But she obviously doesn't care if I feel that way.

"I'll get us some supper, Jackie," my mother says. She's been looking at me strangely and I realize I've been daydreaming for a long time.

"Forget it. I'm not hungry," I snap. "I'm going to bed." I run to my room and close the door. I wait to see if she'll follow me, to try to find out why I'm angry. But she doesn't. She's probably thinking about her bone marrow, hoping it'll contain the magic ingredients Theresa needs to live. Meanwhile, my stomach is gurgling with hunger. I lie on my bed and listen to it rotating. I feel like it's sending me a message, if only I could decipher it. It occurs to me that maybe I need to reconnect with healthy people, people my own age. Maybe I'm getting too wrapped up in Theresa. Thank God Katie's coming back next weekend. She's been gone longer than she said she would be. I'll tell her everything about Theresa. I'm sure she'll understand. And with her back, we can start hanging out with our gang again. I realize I haven't seen anyone my own age except Theresa all summer … well, apart from Alex.

Then I decide to do something I've never done before — call Alex at his dad's. I need to hear his voice, to remember that there is a place beyond Theresa's and Nicole's where I used to belong, where I might still belong.

"Is Alex there, please?" I say when a grown man, most likely his father, answers. He says, "Just a sec," and puts the phone down.

"Hi, Alex," I say when he comes on the line.

"Hey, babe," he says, his voice all sexy. "I'm really sorry I didn't show up last night. I tried, but my dad wanted us to watch this video together and…" My heart sinks.

"Alex, what are you talking about?" There's a long, silent pause.

"Jackie?"

"Who did you think I was?"

"I don't know. I was supposed to meet a bunch of people last night, and ... it doesn't matter. Why are you calling me?"

"I wanted to know if you missed me," I say.

"What?"

"I miss you, Alex," I say. I can't believe I said that. It's obviously pointless.

"Jackie, is this a joke or something?"

"What? No, it's not a joke." In my mind, I hear Alex laughing, telling whoever he stood up last night that his deranged ex-girlfriend, the frigid one, called to say she missed him.

"It's okay, Alex, never mind. I'll see you, maybe." Then I hang up. I know I won't see him again, not after that. I blew it before today anyway, I guess, at his house. I was too difficult. Like I said, Alex is used to winning. I'll be the one bridge that collapsed under him, shattering into a million brittle bones.

Chapter 15

That Sunday I know what I want to do. The minute my father and I walk through Nicole's front door I announce, "I want a tattoo." Nicole and my father just look at me and then at each other, their eyes wide. I guess this isn't what they were expecting, not after last Sunday's slip about being together for six months. They probably thought I'd never want to go to Nicole's again. In a way they're right. Except that Nicole has something I want and this is the only way I can get it.

"Well, your little girl has changed her mind at last. What made you decide?" Nicole finally says.

"It doesn't matter, does it? I just want one." I can't explain it to her. And I don't really think I should have to. It's my business why I suddenly want a tattoo. I didn't want a tattoo at first because of my mother. I didn't want her to see the mark of my father's new girlfriend on my skin. But if my mother wouldn't mind giving Theresa her bone marrow, why should I mind giving Nicole my skin?

Before I know it, I'm seated in one of the tomato-red chairs that my father reupholstered. Nicole is seated in a chair above me, looking like a dentist in her white lab coat, which is splattered with colour. My father doesn't join us. He says it can be a girls' thing and goes off to watch the baseball game on TV.

"So, *qu'est-ce que tu veux*, what do you want, chérie?" Nicole asks. She has a pile of binders with stencils for me to choose from, but I already know what I want.

"A butterfly," I say.

"Ah, *un papillon*. Very nice. I have a very pretty one." She opens a binder and shows me a colourful butterfly, just the right size to go below the bikini line on my belly, so that I can keep it hidden.

"*Maintenant*, take off your pants, but just roll down your panties." I feel odd undressing in front of her, but she turns away and afterward says I can put a towel over myself if I want to, which I do. I lie back and close my eyes, preferring not to see what Nicole is doing. I feel her swab my skin with alcohol.

"You don't have much hair, but it's better if I shave it first. It's cleaner, okay?"

"Go ahead," I say. Nicole's the tattoo artist, not me. The razor tickles as it drags across my belly. I imagine it peeling delicate hairs from my skin, making way for the insect. From the corner of my eye, I peek as she inserts a sterilized needle into its drill-like holder and pours different coloured ink into four plastic cups. A larger fifth cup she fills with water from a jug. Then I feel her rubbing some ointment onto my belly and pressing down on the stencil, which she ran through a machine first. When she peels it back, she tells me to take a deep breath, but to relax and keep breathing. It will only hurt for a minute. Then she begins to prick me and fill in the outline of the butterfly. I wince each time the needle pierces my skin, drawing blood. I feel the wings take shape and the creature's body grow in the middle. Every now and then she stops to ask me if I'm okay.

I soon relax a bit and get into the rhythm of the scraping needle filling in the butterfly. I let my imagination wander. I see myself at the hospital, strapped to a narrow table. I imagine the needle going much deeper, down into my pelvic bone, sucking out the marrow. I picture the bone being sucked so dry it crumbles inside my body like old paper, turning to dust.

Nicole is draping a cold towel on my forehead. "Jackie, Jackie," I can hear her say as she gently shakes me. She rarely says my name, and when she does she pronounces the "J" so softly, more like a "sh" sound. It's hypnotic.

"What happened?"

"Don't worry, chérie. You passed out. I've seen it happen to three-hundred-pound men, and much sooner, too. You did well." Nicole is holding my hand and stroking my hair. I look down at my belly to see that it is covered in a hot towel.

"Let it sit for a bit. I'll be back in a few minutes. I'll bring you some cold water."

I want to peek under the towel to see my new skin, but I'm too afraid. Drops of blood have seeped through the terry cloth. When Nicole returns she gives me the water, and as I'm drinking it, she peels the towel off gently and puts some ointment over the tattoo. She puts a strip of gauze over it so that I can get dressed, and tells me I'll need to keep the tattoo covered for twelve hours. She hands me a tube of ointment and instructs me to rub some on the tattoo twice a day. I should also let the air at it as much as possible.

"It'll only really look good in a week, so don't be discouraged, okay? It'll be a butterfly, I promise. Right now, it's a wound." A wound that will heal, unlike Theresa's, I think as I watch Nicole clean my blood from her needles.

I hold my hand over the spot where my new tattoo is seared into my skin. I feel good inside knowing I've done something my mother won't like. A part of Nicole is now permanently etched into my skin. Even if she and my father split up, I'll always carry a piece of her around with me — forever.

Chapter 16

The CD that Theresa's old choir made is playing. It's all classical music, nothing I've ever heard before. Theresa listens with her eyes closed, humming along in parts. During a particularly long soprano section, she says, "That's where I would have come in. My voice was high, really high, you would have heard it. Can you hear the song's a bit flat now? Good, but flat. They'd need me to really spice it up, take it up a notch. Like the Spice Girls without Ginger, eh?"

I have learned that Theresa doesn't necessarily need or want her questions answered. She just likes asking them. When the CD ends, the room grows very quiet. Then Theresa breaks the silence. "The radiation is better than chemo any day, let me tell you. Chemo sucks. Radiation is much easier. You don't feel a thing. And it doesn't make me throw up, just tired. Like when we walked all the way to the corner. I didn't think I could do it. I guess it was dumb, but I really wanted to try. Do you think my hair is starting to grow back yet? What's your guess?"

I shake my head.

"Ha! You're wrong. Look!" and before I know it, she has pulled off her wig. Her head is covered in little prickly hairs, sort of dark blond, no more than a millimetre long. "What do you think? Do you think I look like a porcupine, or what?"

I don't know what to say, so I say nothing. Then we are both quiet for a while. Theresa isn't dressed up this time, either. She's in the sweatsuit I threw her last week. I don't know if it's my imagination, but her cheeks seem to have a bit of colour today. Maybe it was the walk in the sun. She looks better — to me. We won't be doing that today, though. I was surprised when my mother said Theresa's mother wanted me to visit again.

"I showed you something. Now, you show me," she says suddenly.

"What?"

"I showed you something, now it's your turn."

I want to tell her that I don't do show and tell anymore, but I feel I can't refuse her. She seems so excited. I wasn't going to come back here anymore after my mother announced she was going to become a possible bone marrow donor, but in the end I couldn't stay away. I kept seeing Theresa's face before we took the walk. She looked so happy. And later, stroking the fur on the caterpillar. If I hadn't come over that day, she would have spent it indoors, with her curtains drawn.

"I guess you're not used to doing this, but I am. It's how me and the other kids passed the time in the hospital. Believe me, you have to find ways of doing that. So, at night, when the nurses were out of the room, we would show each other things."

"What things?"

"You know, *things.*" The way she emphasizes the word makes it seem loaded. "Scars from operations, weird birthmarks, needle marks, IV marks, body parts. Double-jointed tricks, eyeball spins. *Things.*"

I haven't shown my tattoo to anyone yet. If I show it to Theresa, she'll be the first. I wanted Katie to be the first tomorrow, but whatever! It's still not completely healed, but it's pretty close. I stand up and close her door. I can hear the vacuum cleaner running in the hall, on its way down toward Theresa's room. I unzip my jeans and pull the flaps down until I can see the rim of my underpants. Then I stand right next to Theresa so that she can get a good view and pull the elastic of my underpants down until the butterfly emerges. It has a long body coloured blue, with two wispy antennae reaching toward my belly button. Four diamond-shaped wings extend two inches across my belly. They are done in black outline, filled in with red and green stripes. Nicole circled the whole thing with red dots, probably when I was passed out because I don't remember feeling the pokes.

Theresa's eyes widen. "Wow! It's beautiful.

When did you get it? Did your mother actually let you? I don't know anyone your age who has a real tattoo. My mother would never let me, even if I wasn't sick. She'd definitely never let me now. Not with the germs and the possibility of infection. It's so cool, I love it. You must show it off to everyone. Your friends must be so jealous."

"Actually, you're the only one I've shown it to."

Theresa's eyes widen in their large sockets. "I am?"

"Ya." I zip up my jeans.

"How come?" She runs her hand over the peach fuzz on her scalp as if to make sure it's still there.

"I don't know. I guess I was afraid I'd have to get rid of it if anyone saw it." I picture the butterfly lifting off my skin and flying away.

"But what about your boyfriend? He must've seen it right? I can just see you exposing it like you did with me. That would make him go nuts, right?"

I can't understand why Theresa thinks I have such an exciting love life. Then I remember that she gets all her impressions about teen romance from the music videos she loves to watch, those and movies. No wonder she has it wrong. Alex and I aren't even a couple anymore. If he did come to Montreal last weekend, he never called me. This is one butterfly he'll never see.

"I don't have a boyfriend anymore, Theresa. I never really did."

"But you said you did."

"Well, I thought I did, kind of. But it just didn't work out. So forget it. You're the only one who's seen my tattoo. But don't tell anyone, okay? You're right. My mother would kill me."

"Cross my heart and hope to die," she replies, doing the actions. I wince inside, trying not to let her see, when she says those last three words. How can she say them so casually, as if they don't mean anything to her?

"I trust you, don't worry," I add. I don't want her to feel she has to make such a deep promise, one that she'd be willing to die to keep.

When her mother comes in to tell her it's time for a nap, I can see my mother vacuuming. If she had seen the tattoo she'd be attacking it now with the hose, trying to lift it off of me, especially if she forced me to confess who gave it to me.

But my butterfly is safe in its underwear cocoon, for now.

Chapter 17

My father and Nicole are away in Cape Cod for the week. My father called Saturday night to tell me that the trip was a last-minute thing and that he hoped I understood why he and Nicole needed to go alone.

"It'll be our test flight," he said. "A whole week together — night and day. It'll either make or break us." I found that strange, since he's practically moved in to Nicole's. I think he still has his basement apartment, but I've never seen it. It also seems strange to me that he'd take Nicole to Cape Cod, the one place we'd gone on family vacations for many years when I was little. Why not go somewhere different, somewhere without those associations?

"Okay. Good luck," I said. What else can you say to a father who's telling you the week will either make him closer to his new girlfriend or bust them up altogether?

And now, on Sunday, I'm left with the daunting task of explaining to my mother why I'm not spending the day with my father.

"He's away," I tell her when she asks.

"Away where?" she asks.

"I don't know. He didn't tell me. Just away." My mother can tell I'm covering up, but for some reason she doesn't push. She just shrugs and walks off, carrying a large load of dirty work clothes into the basement.

The whole weekend would have been very long, except that Katie is back in town. She calls me at ten and I bike over. I have a lot to tell her about. And I can't wait to show her my tattoo. Katie and I have been friends since Grade 4, our last year of elementary school. It's a case of opposites attracting. Where I'm quiet, Katie's outspoken. Where I kind of wait to see what everyone else wants to do before voicing my opinion, Katie just speaks her mind. Where I wouldn't have the nerve in a million years to walk up to some guy I have a crush on and introduce myself, Katie will do just that, without any hesitation.

We're sitting on Katie's bed. She's still unpacking. While putting her clothes and things in piles, she tells me about her trip to Nova Scotia. Her aunt lives close to a really great beach and Katie's skin has turned a golden brown. I'm like a loaf of white sliced bread next to her. My tan from Long Sault is long gone.

"I met this really great guy named Tod," she

says. I should have expected it. That explains why she stayed away longer than she was supposed to. "It'll be a long-distance relationship. But that's okay 'cause he's so gorgeous. And he has two more years of high school to do in Nova Scotia, then he's going to apply to McGill and Concordia so that he can move to Montreal."

I quickly calculate Tod's age in my head. He must be around seventeen, even older than Alex. I wonder if Katie's worried about that. He might want even more from her than Alex did from me. But if she is worried, she doesn't let it show. She's so excited I don't want to tell her about Alex, but she'll find out anyway, so I should.

"Alex and I kind of broke up," I say, twisting my hair around my index finger to make the statement seem more casual.

"Oh my God! Why? What happened?" Katie stops sorting and sits beside me on the bed.

"I don't know. Nothing really happened. It just kind of didn't work out, you know?" It strikes me that this explanation sounds painfully similar to the one my mother gave me when I asked her about my father leaving. I hope that doesn't mean I have some biological gene that's going to predispose me to drifting apart from every guy I go out with.

"That sucks," Katie says. She says it in a matter-of-fact tone, as though she's more surprised than concerned. It was Katie, after all, who got me and Alex together.

"It's okay, I'm not really mad or anything," I

106

respond, hoping she won't ask me to explain. For some reason, I'm hesitant to tell her that Alex basically wants a girlfriend who doesn't push him away whenever he gets horny. He needs a girl who's not shy or scared. Who doesn't mind being rushed into things. It's hard to imagine Katie getting into a mess like that. She'd be the one calling the shots. Kind of like Nicole. I realize that Katie doesn't even know about Nicole. I only found out about her after Katie left. I haven't had any contact with Katie, either by snail mail or by e-mail. Our computer's still at my father's shop.

I also want to tell Katie about Theresa, but I don't really know how to bring her up. Katie knows her the same way I used to, as that sick girl who appears outside from time to time, dressed up in party clothes. The only time they were ever in the same room was probably at my tenth birthday party. Does it make me sound kind of pathetic to confess that I lost my hot boyfriend but befriended the sick girl this summer? Will she really understand?

"His family just kind of adopted me," Katie says. For a second, I don't know what she's talking about. Then I realize she's already forgotten Alex. Her head is too full of Tod. "They want me to come back at Christmas. My parents seem cool about it. I guess 'cause my mom's sister knows his mother so well. They live in the same town."

"That's great, Katie." She pulls out a pack of pictures. They're all of her and Tod making different poses at the beach. In each one they have their arms draped around each other. He's a lot taller than Katie. In a couple of shots he's picking her up. He makes her look light as a feather. The expression on Katie's face is pure bliss. She looks like she's being lifted straight up to heaven. My heart sinks. I don't know why. Did I ever really expect to feel that way about Alex? It was other people who were so excited when he asked me out. I felt I couldn't say no. But I never really felt that much for him.

"Do you remember Theresa?" I ask suddenly. If I wait for the perfect opening, I'm never going to tell her. "The sick girl across the street?"

"Yeah, what about her?"

"Well, I've kind of gotten to know her a bit over the summer. She's all right," I say, a little too defensively.

"How did *that* happen?"

Great! Now I have to tell her about my mother's job. "Well, my mother is cleaning her house now, so I just started going over with her every now and then, and I got to know Theresa."

Katie's face falls. I know how it all sounds. Alex dumping me, my mother cleaning houses, and me with no one better to hang with than the sick girl. I feel like crawling under Katie's bed.

"Well, I'm here now, so you can get back to normal," she says. Something about the way Katie says "normal" bothers me. Does having a friend who's sick make me abnormal? That kind of implies that there's something abnormal about

Theresa. It's true that being sick makes her different, but not abnormal. Being sick isn't her fault. Besides, why does Katie get to decide what normal is? Is it just because she's always so sure of herself, sure of what she needs to make her life perfect, like this new guy Tod? She thought Alex would make my life great, and look how wrong she got that one.

I suddenly remember my butterfly. It's probably the most exciting thing that's happened to me this summer. I thought I'd show it to Katie right away. It's the one thing that could put her in awe of me. But I can't reveal it now. It would seem pathetic, like I was trying to score points and undo the damage of Alex and Theresa.

"We have a whole month of summer left to get you back on track," Katie is saying. "Maybe we can work on getting you and Alex back together."

"Forget it, Katie. He's not even here. He's at his dad's. I've only seen him twice all summer."

"So, that's no reason to split up. Don't worry. I'll fix you up."

"Sure Katie," I say. "Whatever!" There's absolutely no point in arguing with Katie, not when she's begun scheming.

Chapter 18

I wake up Monday morning thinking about Theresa lying on her bed across the street, watching MuchMusic or Spice World for the thousandth time. I don't know how she can stand it.

Katie had some plan to come over today and help coach me through another phone call with Alex where I get him to invite the two of us to his father's. That's the last place I'd want to go right now. I know he wouldn't want me there. I'm sure he has a new girlfriend in Ontario.

My only hope is to not be here when Katie calls. She's one of those people you just can't say no to. So what the heck? Theresa's over there all alone and I need place to hide out for a while. My mother will think I'm Little Miss Wonderful, and Theresa and I can help each other pass the time.

My mother's already over there, so this will be my first totally unannounced visit. I ring the bell and a minute later Theresa's mother answers. She looks surprised. "Jackie?" she exclaims.

"Hi, Mrs. Desjardins. I was wondering if I could visit Theresa? I brought some music," I say. I hold up my stack of CDs to prove it. She looks a bit worried, but lets me in anyway. I don't see my mother but I can hear the vacuum cleaner running somewhere.

Theresa is lying on her bed watching TV. I thought she'd be excited about seeing me, but if she is she's not showing it.

"I brought some of my CDs along, if you want to listen to them," I say. "I've got the Black Eyed Peas and Simple Plan and Michelle Branch, a real mix of styles. I didn't know which one you'd like."

"First I want to see your tattoo," Theresa says, surprising me with the bluntness of her request. So, once again I close her door and reveal the butterfly on my belly.

I expect her to gasp and bubble away, like she did the last time, but she doesn't. She says absolutely nothing as she looks at the tattoo. She's studying the butterfly almost as if she's memorizing its colour.

"Do you think it looks more settled in than last time?" I ask. "I think it does. I find that the colours have deepened, like they've finally sunk in."

Theresa just shrugs.

"I wish she'd put a bit more red on this wing," I say, pointing to the left wing of the insect. I'm just making conversation really, trying to open

Theresa up. If she knew how bad I am at conversation she'd probably appreciate my effort more.

Instead of opening her up, my question seems to shut her off. She turns her head away from me and stares at the white wall intently, as though it's a projection screen filled with images that only she can see.

I'm starting to think that maybe I shouldn't have come. Perhaps Theresa does need lead time for visits, to get psyched up.

When she turns back to face me, her expression is cold. "The colour is fine, you know. There's nothing wrong with it. I don't know what you're complaining about," she blurts out, pulling herself up on her elbows. I've never seen her so angry.

"Sorry, I didn't mean to upset you."

Theresa just mumbles something that sounds like "forget it." Then she switches the channel to MuchMusic. We sit in silence watching music videos with their flashy, quick-paced, colourful scenes. Theresa's eyes are riveted to the screen. I have the feeling she would enjoy the videos just as much with the sound down, like I do. It's the images that are holding her captive.

We don't say another word to each other for the whole visit. The CDs I brought are sitting untouched on the bureau. I'm kind of disappointed. I thought I'd brighten up her day, but I just messed it up instead.

Eventually I tune out, not following the music videos at all. I'm actually relieved when Theresa's mother comes in and tells me it's time to go home. I turn back at the door and watch her pull the beige cover up over Theresa's thin body.

I think I see her shrivel up under it, like a caterpillar that's been poked by a finger.

Chapter 19

There won't be any way out of this one. Katie called this morning to say that she had it all arranged. I held my breath. Katie's arrangements are like whirlwinds. You get caught up in them whether you want to or not. She actually had the nerve to call Alex in Ontario. She somehow got him to confess that he's going to be back in town this weekend and that he'll be at a party at his friend Paul's tonight. I know Paul. I spent a lot of time in the spring sitting in his basement watching Alex and his friends play pool. Paul has lots of electric guitars lying around, and in between pool shots he'd pick one up and try to play along to whatever ancient heavy metal song was blaring on his sound system. I don't think he's ever said more than five words to me.

"So, we can go and meet Alex there," Katie said. How could I tell her I didn't want to? I felt the same way I did that horrible day at Alex's, when he had me half undressed on his bed. Caught, without a voice to get myself out of it.

So, here I am, trying to decide what to wear to the party Katie and I are crashing at Paul's. She ordered me to wear something sexy. She'll be here any minute to check me out. The trouble is, my clothes don't really fall into the category of sexy. I don't own any super-tight miniskirts or clingy halter tops. I'm a jeans and T-shirt sort of girl. I don't even like exposing my midriff, like every pop star on the planet does. I have a sudden picture of Theresa out on her front deck in her party gear the day my father left. That's exactly the kind of outfit Katie has in mind for me, tight and sparkly. I wonder if Theresa would lend it to me if I called her? If she's in the same mood she was in last time I saw her, she probably wouldn't even speak to me.

Suddenly Katie's here. "You can't wear that!" she shrieks when she sees me in my tightest jeans and a plain black but fairly tight T-shirt. I even put five different necklaces on and a bright red belt with silver studs to jazz it all up.

"You have to show him something, Jackie, if you want him to drop dead with regret for letting you go." Then she starts rifling through my drawers. She pulls up a blue shirt with *spaced out* written in sequins across the front. "This is old, right? So you don't mind if we operate on it?"

I shrug my shoulders. Then I watch in amazement as Katie takes a pair of scissors out of my desk drawer and begins to chop at the shirt. First, she scoops out the neck so that it's about five inches wider than it was before. Then she chops the sleeves off, one to mid arm the other almost at the shoulder. Next she folds the front of the shirt in half, below the writing, and cuts out an oval shape over the belly. Finally, she shortens it by a couple of inches by cutting off the bottom in jagged lines. It looks like a shirt that got caught in a lawn mower.

"Voila," she says. "That's better. Now, don't you even own a short skirt?" I shake my head. Katie opens my closet door and starts rummaging around. "What are these?" she asks, pulling a pair of jeans out of a heap on the floor.

"Old jeans," I say. "They're way too tight."

"Perfect! Here, put them on." She throws the old jeans onto my shoulder. I turn around and take off the jeans I'm wearing. As I stand there, facing away from Katie, I think how easy it would be to show her my butterfly. The top ring of red dots that circle the insect are visible above my panties. Katie would be so impressed. But I don't do it. I have a strong feeling that my butterfly needs to remain hidden. If Katie sees it, she'll want to use it somehow in her scheme to win Alex back. She'll cut a hole in my jeans and underwear to expose it. But that's not what my butterfly is for.

I can barely breathe in the old jeans, not unless I stick to short, choppy puffs. "Those look fantastic," Katie says. "They really show you off." I look in my dresser mirror. They sure do show me off. I'm practically bursting out of them. There is a line at my crotch where the material slices into me. Alex will love that! And because the pants are low and the T-shirt is now cropped a few inches shorter, a rim of stark white stomach is sticking out.

I feel like a carefully constructed fishing lure, especially after Katie is finishing colouring me up with blue eyeshadow and pink lipstick. She wants to pull my black hair up into a high, striking ponytail, the kind that pulls your eyes back into the shape of a cat's, but I put my foot down.

"No way, Katie. I want my hair down. Ponytails give me headaches," I lie. At least my curtain of hair will give me somewhere to hide.

Katie pulls me downstairs by the arm. We call goodbye to my mother, who is talking to her sister on the phone in the kitchen. Katie remarked earlier tonight that my mother was looking sharp. "She's lost a lot of weight and looks more alive," is how she put it. I could've explained how taking care of Theresa and even cooking for her now has rejuvenated my mother, but I just let it go.

We head up the street to Paul's, taking the same route to the corner that I took with Theresa a few weeks ago. Only this time I'm the one being led, leaning into Katie's body as she pulls me toward Alex.

Chapter 20

We can hear the bass of the music pumping out the sides of the house as we approach. Lots of cars are parked on either side of the street, several of them with Ontario licence plates. I want to turn around and run home, but Katie is so determined. Her hand is hooked under my arm now and she's leading me up the path. The front door opens and a few people I don't know spill out. They crack up and take off around the side of the house.

Inside, the party is in full swing. Groups of kids are scattered everywhere, some standing, most sitting on the floor or draped over furniture. Almost everyone is holding a beer bottle. The lights are either out or low so that I feel like I'm walking through a misty cave, the mist being the blend of tobacco and weed smoke. The racket of voices that are yelling and singing slices through my brain. God even knows where Alex is in all this.

Katie is still pulling me, only this time by the

hand. She is two or three bodies ahead of me so that I am like the tail end of a kite. We end up in the kitchen. Paul sees us.

"Hey, Katie," he calls over the music, looking her up and down. Katie is, of course, perfectly dressed, exactly the way she wanted me to dress: tight and short. But then again, Katie always looks fantastic. Now that she has this older boyfriend, she's even more self-assured. It doesn't seem to bother her that Paul's eyes are hanging out of their sockets. She's even posing to make it easy for him. Then, when she's had enough, she turns away. Paul just sort of nods at me. I always got the feeling that Paul couldn't figure out why Alex chose to hang out with me, not when half the girls in their own grade would've jumped at the chance.

Katie helps herself to two beers sitting in a bucket of ice in the sink. She hated beer, like me, before she went away. Did Tod teach her to like it?

"It'll help us blend in," she shouts into my ear, twisting off the caps.

Katie sidles up to Paul, who has gone back to staring at her again. "Is Alex here?" I hear her shout. Paul nods, but when Katie asks where he is, he just shakes his head and waves his hand around, as if to say he could be anywhere.

So we start our tour, room by room, wandering in and out, looking for Alex. This party has invaded every space in the house. A couple of girls are doing a weird dance on top of the coffee table, making wings of their arms and buzzing like bees, a crowd cheering them on. In the den, a strip poker game is well under way, with a couple of guys stripped to boxer shorts and one girl clinging protectively to her bra. Whenever we enter a room people stare at us for a while, but then they lose interest. I think I must be one of the youngest people here.

In the basement, a wild game of pool is under way. People are whacking balls like crazy, in any order, sometimes just rolling them by hand without the cue. Several bottles are balanced on the edge of the table and when people lean against the table they wobble. Paul's parents will kill him if they spill. He's normally so careful about his precious table. He doesn't let anyone smoke while playing so that a stray ember can't fall down and burn a hole in the felt. But I guess he's pretty drunk now, so he doesn't care.

Katie pulls me down beside her on the carpet. She whispers hoarsely in my ear that maybe we should stay put and sooner or later he'll show up. It's just like being lost in the woods, I think. You're supposed to stay put and hug a tree and wait for the rescuers. That's fine with me. I lean back as far as I can into the wall, where the dark hides me.

A couple of guys have the electric guitars going, except none of them can play. Their notes are all random, like the billiard balls. The far corner has turned into a kind of dance floor and people are actually trying to dance to the weird blend of off-key notes and actual music, some techno-pop stuff. I stare at the twisting and jerking bodies, thinking how I could never just get up and dance like that in front of everyone. I wouldn't have the guts. But I bet they wouldn't either if they weren't full of beer and marijuana.

Maybe that's the key to not caring and letting yourself go free, to not being afraid.

I turn to Katie and realize that's she actually already finished her beer. She's tapping the empty with her long nails, trying to add her own bit of rhythm to the noise.

I take a sip of my beer. It tastes like old socks or bitter medicine. But I keep drinking it anyway. I use the twisting happy bodies across from me as my inspiration. I want to turn myself into that. I want to unfold myself and spring into action, moving my body as freely as they are. Maybe Katie has the right idea. When Alex sees me and notices how loose and happy I look, he'll regret dumping me. I'll tuck myself right into the middle of the dancing crowd, as though I truly belong, like Katie. I gasp. Katie really is one of them. I look beside me. Sure enough, she's not there. That is her, over on the dance floor.

I have half a bottle of beer to go and then I can join them. What will I do with my bottle when it's empty? I suppose I could dance with it, like many people are, waving their bottles around like miniature dance partners.

I'm working on pulling myself up. I wish I really was hugging a tree. Then I'd have something to hold on to. I'm sort of suspended on my knees now, hoping the rotating gurgle in my stomach will calm down and I can pull myself upright. I glance over at the dance floor. Paul is now dancing beside Katie. I guess he's given up on trying to save his pool table. Behind Paul, flailing his arms around as though he's riding a log on a river, is Alex. I'm sure it's him. His hair is even longer than it was a month ago and he has it pulled into a ponytail that hits his neck as he dances.

Why isn't Katie trying to bring him over here? She's just happily dancing beside him as though that was why we came here in the first place. This whole mission was her idea. She's the one who thinks we should get back together. I wish she'd at least look at me and send me a signal, let me know what I should do next.

I guess I should join them. I suppose it's up to me to step out of this dark corner and join the group. Katie's done what she can. She dressed me and pulled me here. I suppose the rest is up to me.

I take a deep breath and stand, bracing my free hand against the wall. The whoosh in my stomach is like a wave. My head is dizzy. I stand for a minute, letting everything settle.

I can do this. I look great, I remind myself. Katie was right. Every single snip and cut has turned this shirt into a piece of boy bait. I just need to get close to Alex and start moving. He'll remember what he liked about me. How I don't overwhelm his space and just kind of blend into it.

How he could do things to me without too much protest, like yanking off my bra, twice. And I'll wave my long dark hair around. Alex always liked my hair. I have a sudden flash of Nicole that first day at the beach, the way she tossed her own long hair over her shoulder before taking off down the sand to the water.

I start across the room. It's like the pool table is a large plateau and the bodies on the dance floor are a forest in the middle of a hurricane.

What does that make me? I'm a deer. A delicate deer taking its first steps on long, wobbly legs.

But I'm almost there. The swirl in my stomach has now hardened into a tight knot. I keep my eyes ahead on my destination: Katie, Paul, and Alex. Alex is facing away from me now. Something strange is happening to his back. It's like his arms have become double-jointed and are now draped around his own waist. He turns. He is laughing, throwing his head back so that his ponytail is flying loose in the air.

It's a girl. Her arms are wrapped around Alex's body. I stop dead in my tracks.

Katie sees me. She's waving. No, she's waving me over. It doesn't seem to matter to her that Alex, the main target of this mission, is wrapped like a pretzel around some girl I've never seen before. She must be from Ontario. She's probably the one who called his house the time he said he wasn't doing anything. Lying around half-naked with me was doing nothing, for Alex. I guess he didn't care, 'cause he'd be going back to the new girl anyway. Maybe they make out in the shed Alex is helping his dad build. I guess she doesn't fuss and try to push him off the way I did. Their two bodies do seem to fit together, like some well-constructed, interlocking structure, like a drawbridge.

I'm standing there completely stunned. Suddenly, I have no idea what to do. Katie's still waving. It seems she wants me to just forget it all and come over and dance and have a good time. I can hear her telling me that I take everything too seriously. But then I remind myself that I didn't even want to come here in the first place. I don't care about losing Alex. I had no real connection to him. I don't think I really wanted to go out with him in the first place.

As I head for the stairs, I wonder about my parents. Is that why they split up? Because they felt no connection to each other anymore? It makes sense. You can't fake connection. My father has it now with Nicole, even though it's a hard one for me to understand.

I fight my way along the hallway, stepping over and around, and sometimes on, people. The two bumblebees are still buzzing on the table. I can see the front door up ahead, dimmed by smoke. I have to practically shove a necking couple out of the way to open it, but they don't seem to notice. I float down the front stairs, light as a feather on my feet. Then I float through the dark streets of the neighbourhood. It's so quiet. I'm not aware of steering myself at all, as if I'm on an invisible conveyor belt. As I move, I think about how Katie thought the party would reignite my romance with Alex and make me normal again. I look down at the shirt she fashioned for me, my white skin flashing through the holes. I don't feel more united — just more cut off.

Suddenly, I'm standing in front of Theresa's house. I have an urge to knock on her window and wake her up. I could tell her about the party. She'd like that. I have a mental image of her outside in her party clothes, looking scared and eager all at once, soaking up the sun, pretending she was part of the world, probably feeling that she was missing out on some exciting life where people our age go to parties and have hot boyfriends and loads of nothing but fun all the time.

The happy world of a music video.

Before I know it, I'm doing something really strange. It's like I have no control over my legs. I'm sailing up the stairs to Theresa's deck. I can't do this. I can't ring her bell this late at night. Her mother would kill me. But then I stop and plunk myself down on a chair, one of the two I put out here for me and Theresa weeks ago. No one has bothered to put them back.

I lean back and look up at the sky. Only a few stars are visible under the clouds and pollution. The moon is just a sliver, like a fingernail clipping. It's so peaceful here. The bass of the music is still thumping, trapped by my eardrums, tapping like wings against glass. Behind it is the melodic sound of crickets, rubbing their legs together like violins.

Behind the stone wall, Theresa is asleep in her bedroom. I close my eyes and see her room, spinning slightly. I see the white walls, beige curtains, and beige bedspread. I see, as though for the first time, how sterile her world is — swept and washed free of germs on a daily basis. Life in a permanent cocoon, without any spot of colour. Even Theresa's clothes are white. And her body is part of the picture, too, her pale skin so transparent that her veins shine through. And inside those veins the white cells are racing around her blood outnumbering the red. Even her disease is one of colour.

It's as though I'm seeing all this clearly for the first time, sitting here under the skinny moon. Now I understand why Theresa got so angry the other day when I complained about the colour of my tattoo, when I said the red wasn't red enough. I made it sound dull, when to her it must seem to be bursting with brightness.

Suddenly, the weight of Theresa's illness hits me, as though the stone facade of her house is crumbling on top of me. Theresa might die. And she is my friend. She's someone I care about, more than about Katie or Alex. More than just about anyone right now.

All the best moments of this summer have involved Theresa — sitting in her room, listening to her stories about being sick, seeing the hair start to grow back on her head, watching her face grow excited when I showed her my tattoo or told her about my life, watching her amazed face as she stroked the caterpillar.

I think about the bright orange caterpillar again. I thought she was drawn to its fur. But now I know I was wrong. It was the colour. I should have known. The whole summer has been about gaining colour. My father gained it with Nicole, my mother with her job, which has taken her back to her happy, active days as a nurse's aide. Nicole's given me some colour, too, with my tattoo.

Theresa's the only one who has no colour, so far.

I look across the street at my house. It looks like it's sleeping, all the blinds drawn over the windows like eyelids. My mother's tucked into her bed, the one she used to share with my father. My father's probably tucked into bed beside Nicole at some beachfront cabin, listening to the rolling waves. Katie's probably still on the dance floor, shining. Everyone's in their proper place.

Suddenly, I know what I need to do.

I carry my plan down the stairs and into my own house, tucking it deep into my brain as I slip into bed and fall asleep.

Chapter 21

I wake up thinking of Alex and Ontario girl locked together, Katie dancing beside them as if they were all friends. But the image doesn't really bother me. It's quickly cancelled out by thoughts of my plan, which I am going to start to execute today.

"Your father called," my mother tells me in the kitchen. "He'll be here at ten."

"Oh, thanks." I wait for my mother to say more, but she's intently reading the newspaper, which is spread before her under her coffee mug. I wonder if he told her where he was and with whom. Or did he simply say he was back and coming to get me?

My father shows up at ten, as promised. I'm glad, because I'm eager to get Nicole's help to get my plan underway. We don't talk much in the car. He says they had really nice weather and a really good time. I want to ask if they hung out at the little beach about a ten minute walk from the cabins, sheltered by a thick strand of marsh grass, or if they hiked the boardwalk trail into the marshes where the bird sanctuary is. If I close my eyes, I can almost smell the mixture of ocean salt and marsh water. I used to love going there. But it doesn't seem appropriate to bring up our former trips now.

Nicole has turned a light chocolate brown that makes her even more gorgeous than before. I suppose the trip hasn't broken their relationship. They seem closer than ever. They had a caricature of themselves drawn at the beach and it now hangs over the sofa. In it, their faces are bloated and distorted, with Nicole's long blond hair draped dramatically over my father's near bald dome, but they are smiling broadly at each other inside a circle of red and purple hearts.

"I have to do some work in the shop," Nicole announces shortly after we've arrived. "I have clients tomorrow. I have to clean."

"Can I help?" I say suddenly. Nicole looks from me to my father.

"She wants to help, your little girl, eh? Well, why not? Okay." I follow Nicole into Tattoo Heaven. It looks as red as ever.

"I have to resterilize everything, *c'est très important*," she says.

"I could put your stencils in order. The shelves are kind of messy," I volunteer. I hope I don't seem too eager or she'll get suspicious. I have never volunteered to do anything at Nicole's before.

"*Eh bien,* that would be nice."

The stencils are in binders according to type: animals, hearts, mythological creatures, sexy stuff, machines. I guess that's the one my father's Model T came from. I basically put the loose ones back in the rings and try to refile ones that are in the wrong place. But as I'm doing so, I'm checking them for ones that Theresa might like. I'll also need to pick Nicole's brains on how I could possibly do what I want to do. There's no other way. If I had access to the computer in my father's shop I could do a search on Google.

"Nicole?"

"*Oui, chérie?*"

"Is there any way to give someone a tattoo without the needles, like, just for fun?"

"Well, you could use some skin dye, like henna. Or some paint, *de corps,* for the body," she says.

"Do they stay on the skin for a long time?"

"It depends. Henna, yes, the body paint, no. It washes off. *Pourquoi*? Do you want another tattoo?" Nicole's almond-shaped eyes squint at me as though she's catching on.

"No, no. Just wondering. A friend asked me. Her mother won't let her get a real one, so we thought we'd do a temporary one."

"Ah, *je voix.* You can get temporary tattoos. Some of them are really nice. I have some if you want to see."

"Sure," I say, trying to sound casual. Wow! I didn't think it would be this easy.

Nicole pulls a box off a shelf above the sink. A cloud of dust billows off it and hovers in the air. "I don't use these much, just sometimes for kids, for fun. They only last four or five days." She opens the box and points to a stack of tattoos. There are so many. "You can take whatever you want."

"Thanks." I start to riffle through the pile. Nicole's still standing beside me. I thought she'd go back to her work.

"You know, Jackie," she says suddenly. "What happened with your parents. It had nothing to do with me, *rien de tout*. Your father, he was unhappy when I met him. Maybe he left sooner because of me, but I didn't cause the separation."

I simply nod my head. I could point out that maybe my parents could have worked on getting happy again if she hadn't come along, but I'm not so sure that's even true. Besides, Nicole's being nice giving me these tattoos, I don't want to say anything to upset her.

"Your father, he was unhappy for a long time. It wasn't because he met me that he decided to leave your mother," she continues. She really wants me to believe her. I didn't think it would be that important to her. Is it true that my father was unhappy more than six months ago? I remember my mother saying the silence had just crept in. It's true. The rift was there long before six months ago. It was there whenever my father came home and they barely said two words to each other. It was there when he pushed back on his lounge chair and snapped open the foot rest. It was as though that snap was meant to shut her out, like an exclamation mark.

"Can I have these?" I ask. I hold up a fire-breathing dragon with a cheerful face, an intricate pattern of intertwined hearts circling a kitten, a blue jay and a cardinal kissing on a branch, a colourful mermaid, and an angel with very large blue wings.

"Of course, *chérie*, take whatever you want."

"Thanks," I say. Nicole's a hard person to dislike.

I spend the next hour doing a great job on the binders and then I wash the shelves and rearrange everything in perfect order.

"It looks great. *Merci*," Nicole says. "Let's stop now."

When we enter the livingroom, my father is totally absorbed in a baseball game: the Expos are beating their opponents, for a change, and my father is happy.

"Dad, I think I want to leave early today," I say out of the blue. I figure Sunday would be a good day to see Theresa alone, without my mother hanging around. My father looks surprised. "I can get home myself, on the metro. You don't have to drive me," I say forcefully. Now my father looks a bit embarrassed, as if he's finally realized that he doesn't pay me enough attention.

"That's too bad, Jackie, but if that's what you want," he says kind of sadly. Then he hangs his head down and focuses on his intertwined fingers.

It occurs to me that maybe my father doesn't mean to ignore me. Maybe he's just figuring it all out himself — how to mesh his old life with his new one. How to integrate me with Nicole. After all, it's not like he doesn't want to see me. He's picked me up every Sunday since he left home, except when he was away. I guess I have to remember that this is all new for him, too.

Nicole pops out of the kitchen, where she's started preparing supper.

"Jackie's not staying for supper, honey," my father tells her. Nicole actually looks disappointed. "But she has to stay, your little girl, we have something to give her." Nicole looks at me in a friendly way. "Why don't you stay?" she says. "We haven't seen you for a long time."

"We'd like it if you stayed, Jackie," my father adds. His voice croaks, as though this was really hard for him to say. It's always been hard for him to show emotion. I'm kind of touched by their reaction. I didn't think they'd care if I left early.

"Give her her gift now. Then she can decide," Nicole says. My father pulls a package off the shelf behind the sofa and hands it to me. The wrapping paper is beige, like sand, with seashells on it.

"*Vas-y*. Go on. Open it!" Nicole says. "Don't be shy."

I unwrap the gift. Inside I find a pair of starfish earrings, a ring with a starfish attached to it, and a necklace with two starfish strung into some beads. But they aren't tacky plastic ones. They're silver.

The set is really beautiful and it looks expensive. Nicole insists I try them all on immediately. She even helps me with the necklace hook.

"She looks great, your daughter. Doesn't she?" She looks at my father and makes her eyes go big, as though telling him to agree. I get the feeling that Nicole understands a lot more than my father does about the way I'm feeling. Maybe it's because she was my age not that long ago. She knows I need to hear some kind words from my father every now and then. Maybe she had a distant father, too. Maybe that's why she likes my father. He's like a replacement father for her, one who can give her the praise she never had when she was younger. That would explain a lot of things.

"Of course she looks great. She always does," he says. He keeps his eyes on mine the whole time he says it. I just stand there, with all the shiny starfish hanging off of me, totally amazed. My father's face is even redder now. I don't know why genuine connection is so hard for us, all I know is that it is.

Nicole squeezes my shoulders. "So now you will stay, yes, Jackie? I made something just for you." I guess I'm trapped, so I nod. Nicole busies herself setting the table with the fancy white table-cloth and the candelabras. I wonder if they're for me. Nicole is acting like I'm the guest of honour.

Nicole disappears into the kitchen and returns a while later with a casserole of macaroni and cheese, my favourite. How did she know?

My father must have told her.

Nicole pours wine into all of the elegant glasses, including mine. I can't believe I'm having alcohol two days in a row. Then we all clink glasses. I don't really know what we're toasting. It's nothing as definable as an anniversary. It's more just a mood or a feeling. A connection.

The macaroni and cheese is really good, of course. I eat two helpings and think how I really should show Nicole my tattoo. It's now a full-fledged, colourful butterfly, no more scar.

I think she'd like that.

Chapter 22

My mother isn't sure about letting me come with her today. She doesn't think Theresa will be up to it.

"She was in the hospital all day Friday for tests and I'm sure she'll still be tired, Jackie." I really want to see Theresa. I never made it over yesterday because I only got back from Nicole's at around nine. We played Trivial Pursuit after supper.

"She'll be glad to have someone to talk to for a while," I say. "You're the one who wanted me to become her friend."

At that she relents. "You won't be able to stay long, okay?"

Theresa is even quieter this visit than the last. Whatever they did to her at the hospital, she seems battered. Both her arms are bandaged where they have obviously drawn blood. And she is even paler than usual, as if she's been bleached.

We watch music videos for a while and I wait

for Theresa to ask to see my tattoo. But she never does. She normally starts talking first, but this time I know I'll have to get things going.

"I brought you something," I say finally.

"You what?" She turns slowly away from the TV, tired and weak.

"I brought something for you, something you're going to love." Theresa's eyes brighten a little. I pull out my bag and shake its contents onto her bed.

"What's all this?"

"Here, choose." I hand her the stack of tattoos.

"What are they?"

"Tattoos, silly. I'm going to give you one." I get up and shut the door.

"How are you going to do that? Are you crazy?" Theresa becomes a bit more animated.

"You'll see. Now, choose one. We have to work fast before your mom kicks me out."

Theresa looks perplexed, but flips through the stencils anyway. Her eyes take each one in with a dull expression and I'm disappointed that she isn't more excited. I thought she'd love the mermaid with her aqua blue tail. But then she comes to the angel. She holds it up to the light of the window, as though she wants to see through it. Then her eyes light up. "This one is mine," she says, almost matter-of-factly, handing it to me. It's an elegant angel in a long pink robe with blue, tapered wings and a yellow halo. She has long, flowing red hair that seems to be flying out behind her, and on her feet gold slippers point to the earth below her. It's not the type of cutesy angel you find on Christmas cards, fluttering above baby Jesus in his cradle, or floating around on heavenly clouds. It's way more artistic, like something a French painter would have painted a hundred years ago.

"Okay. Well, you understand it isn't going to be perfect, or professional. It's only a temporary tattoo. But they're supposed to work really well. My father's girlfriend gave it to me. Hopefully your mother won't freak out."

Theresa looks a little unsure, and I'm starting to lose my nerve. I shouldn't have mentioned her mother. I also suddenly wonder if I'm acting like Katie when she cut holes in my shirt and forced me into clothes I didn't really want to wear. Katie and I haven't spoken since then. She's probably waiting for me to call and apologize for leaving early. What if doing this to Theresa has the same result?

"I mean, you want a tattoo, don't you?" I ask. Theresa nods but still says nothing. I remind myself of how fascinated she was by my tattoo when I first showed it to her, how her eyes lit up, how she even asked to see it again. This encourages me.

"Okay." I try to sound peppy. "Now, where do you want it?"

"On my arm, I guess." Theresa holds her right arm up to me. It is bruised in a couple of places, but there's enough space to do the angel. I brought some packets of alcohol swabs to clean her skin, like Nicole said I should. Theresa winces when she sees them.

"Don't worry. I'm not giving you a needle. It's just to clean the skin," I say. Theresa just shrugs again. I get the feeling she's so used to being handled she doesn't even know how to fight it anymore. I wish she'd say something.

"Now, I just need to get a wet washcloth. I'm going to sneak one out of the bathroom, okay?" Theresa nods. It only takes me a minute to accomplish my mission. Luckily I don't run into either of our mothers on the way, although I do hear the sounds of running water down the hall in the kitchen.

"Okay, now I just have to wet it all down and press it really hard for a few minutes. Let me know if I'm hurting you." I can feel Theresa's arm bone under the wet cloth. It feels like if I were to squeeze just a bit harder I'd break it. I hold the cloth there for four minutes, like Nicole instructed.

"That should do it. Ready?" I ask. Theresa nods. I wish she was more excited. I begin to peel off the waxy paper. Theresa's eyes scan the spot lazily, but as the tip of the angel appears, her eyes grow wider. I keep peeling, slowly. Theresa doesn't take her eyes off the angel the whole time. She watches it intensely as it gains shape and colour. I think I hear her gasp a little at the sight of the blue wings. By the time the full angel is revealed, Theresa's mouth is open in a wide and happy smile.

"Well? Like it?" I ask.

Theresa just holds up the angel and stares at it.

Then she flaps her arm like a bird and laughs. She dips it up and down and over and under, every way she can possibly move it, watching the angel fly. The smile on her face is a mile wide. I've never seen her so happy.

I feel incredibly powerful, like I've given her something that no one else could give her. This is the second time I've felt this way with Theresa, and I like it.

"I love it, it's awesome," Theresa says, her eyes glued to the angel. "I can't believe it."

"Well, it's true," I say.

"I think it's even bigger and brighter than your butterfly, isn't it?"

"Oh yeah, much. Look." I expose my butterfly, which is a lot smaller than the angel. "Sweet," Theresa says. I'm not offended by her comparing our tattoos. If it were Katie, I know she'd want hers to be the most impressive. But with Theresa, I think she just wants to have something that makes her special. I can understand that.

"I can't wait to show this off at the hospital," she says. "I have to go back this week sometime, for more tests. They're trying to figure out what to do with me next." I want to ask her what she means by that — I wonder if they're still looking for a donor — but just then the door opens and her mother steps into the room. She takes one look at Theresa's arm and gasps.

"What in the world are you doing? Oh my God, what is that?" She puts her hand up to her mouth, as though she's just seen a tarantula. I watch Theresa shrink into her cloudy mountain of pillows.

"It's just a tattoo," I say. "It's temporary, it'll wash off." Now my mother is standing behind Theresa's mother. She probably heard the panic from wherever she was busy scrubbing.

"Oh, Jackie, what have you done?" she says.

"It's just a tattoo." I look at Theresa. Is she going to defend me? She looks at me as though she wants to, but then the energy just evaporates from her body, leaving her flat.

"Why would you do such a thing?" Theresa's mother asks.

"I … I just wanted to give her some colour. That's all."

"You'd better go. You've worn Theresa out. Go on, just go home," Theresa's mother snaps. My mother is stuffing the extra stencils into the bag and picking up the wet cloth. I can see that a spot of water is staining the sheets.

"Don't worry, Mrs. Desjardins. I'll wash everything," she says to Theresa's mother. Then she hands me the bag and points toward the door, avoiding my eyes.

I glance back at Theresa before leaving. She's looking right at me. It's slight, but it's definitely there. A smile. She raises the angel a couple of inches off the pillow. Then her mother moves between us, blocking my view.

As I cross the street I picture them scrubbing Theresa's arm, trying to rub away the angel, then bleaching her sheets and turning her completely white again. But it doesn't get me down. Not really. I see the colourful angel flying in the sky above Theresa's head. I know that I made her happy. And I know that at the very centre of those few moments was me, nobody else but me.

I made the angel happen.

Chapter 23

My mother is still at Theresa's. We've usually had supper and done the dishes by seven and it's now eight. I've been sitting on my bed, peeking out the window, waiting to see her come across the street. What could she be doing over there? I bet she really is washing all of Theresa's sheets and scrubbing down her entire bedroom, just to get rid of any remnants of the tattoo. I don't get what the big deal is. It's only ink. Are they afraid it's going to seep through her skin and into her blood, screwing it up even more?

All I know is that the longer my mother stays away, the worse it's going to be when she comes home. And if she demands to know where I got the tattoos, I'll have no choice but to tell her.

Finally, at about eight-thirty, I hear her key in the lock. When I was a kid I liked to guess who was coming through the door whenever I heard a key — my father or my mother. There's not much point in doing that now.

Should I go talk to her or just hide in my room? I'm really hungry, and besides, we'll have to air this out either tonight or tomorrow. We can't avoid each other in this house. We're like the last two balls of gum in the plastic bubble of a gum machine.

I find my mother on the sofa, her head in her hands. She barely moves when I walk in.

"Mom?" I say. "Are you okay?"

"Oh, Jackie," she says, her voice cracking the way it does just before she cries. "What a day! Did you *have* to do it today, of all days?" Then she lets out a big, tired sigh.

I sit down next to her. Her hands are folded in her lap and I can smell the laundry detergent on them. They're cracked from all the scrubbing she does over there. Not at all like Nicole's smooth, young hands. I suddenly want to take my mother's hand and hold it. She seems so upset.

"I don't know, Mom. It just kind of seemed right. I felt sorry for Theresa." My mother just nods. I think she can understand that. She's been feeling sorry for Theresa for months. "She seemed so pale and white all the time. And her room looks like the inside of an igloo. I thought a bit of colour would cheer her up."

My mother finally looks at me. Not just at me, but sort of into me, as though she hasn't seen me for a long time. "That's really funny, Jackie. It reminds me of something I haven't thought about for ages."

"What?"

"Well, when I was at college, ages ago, and studying to be a nurse's aide, I used to think about what I really wanted to do, which was to study psychology. Whenever I did my practice sessions at the hospital, I used to think about what would make the patients happy. Not just comfortable or clean, which was my main job, but happy. It didn't take me long to figure out that a kind word, or even helping people hang up pictures from home, would cheer them up. Once, I helped a woman sneak in a dog, a little Shih Tzu, to visit her husband. She said the dog was the most important thing in his life. And she was right. His whole demeanour changed after that, and he got better faster, too."

I can't believe what my mother's telling me. I didn't know anything about this. There must have been a lot of stages in her life that I don't know about.

"How come you didn't become a psychologist, then?" I ask.

"Money, mainly. My parents didn't have it. It was my mother who talked me into doing the nurse's aide course. She said it would be practical. One year and then I'd have a job. What I really wanted to do would have taken me lots more time. I thought I could start earning some money, save, and then study psychology part-time."

"So why didn't you do that?"

She stops speaking for a while, then continues. "Well, first I met your father. And then you came along. And then I didn't really think about doing it anymore." I feel my insides jump when she says that. It's as though having me meant she couldn't do what she really wanted to do.

"So, I guess you kind of regret it now, right?"

"Regret what, Jackie?"

"Having me. Meeting Dad, I mean my father, and having me. It means you couldn't become a psychologist."

"Oh, Jackie." My mother's voice is cracking again. "I didn't mean for it to sound like that. It's just things don't always turn out like we plan, you know?"

"You mean I wasn't planned?"

"Oh no, you were planned. Well, it's not exactly like we said let's have a baby now, but when we got married we knew we wanted to have kids."

She said kids, plural. That's not what she got. "How come you only had me?"

"It's just the way it worked out, Jackie," my mother says, but I know that's not the whole story. It's pretty obvious that being a wife and having kids didn't turn out to be my mother's idea of a perfect life. I wonder how much happier she'd be now if she had pursued her dream of being a psychologist. Maybe she could have done that, then had me.

"Is that why you like taking care of Theresa so much?" I ask.

"What do you mean?"

"Well, you know, it's like being back at work,

doing something important, instead of just being my mother." I say the last two words in a tone that suggests they're throwaway words.

"Being your mother is the most important job I've ever had, Jackie. Taking care of Theresa has been a diversion, but it's not more important than you. It never would be." Then my mother does what I had wanted to do. She takes my hand.

"Today, it was just bad timing, Jackie. Theresa's mother would never have let you, but she just found out this morning that neither she nor Theresa's father are suitable matches. The cousins in Ontario and Manitoba are now being tested at local hospitals. All the ones in Quebec have already been done."

"Are you still going to do it?" I hold my breath. I remember how I felt when she first told me she wanted to. I felt she wanted so badly to be connected to Theresa, more than she wanted to be connected to me. But I understand it more now. The angel tattoo was my own connection to Theresa. Even if it is gone in a few days, or already scrubbed from her skin, it's still the way I've left my mark on her. It's like I shared colour, not marrow, with her. And what's life without colour?

"I don't know. Her mother may not want me to keep cleaning over there after today. She was really angry. She's used to having total control of what happens to Theresa. She told me to take a few days off. Theresa has to go back into the hospital anyway for more tests."

Great! First I prevented my mother from pursuing her dream to be a psychologist and now I've gotten her fired from a job that she really enjoyed. A job that made her feel important. What if she loses heart again and lets herself go? I don't think I could stand to see that happen.

"I'm really sorry, Mom. I didn't know this would happen. I just wanted to make Theresa happy."

"Was she happy?" my mother asks.

"Oh my God, you should've seen her. I've never seen her smile like that, not even the day we went for a walk and she pet the caterpillar." The second the words are out of my mouth I want to trap them and shove them back inside.

"Jackie! What walk? What caterpillar?"

"I took her for a walk to the corner a few weeks ago. She saw a caterpillar and wanted to pet it. It gave her such a thrill, you wouldn't believe it." I expect my mother to yell, to let go of my hand and throw up her own hands and confess that she's had enough and can't take anymore. But instead, she is actually laughing. It starts out as a little giggle, but after a minute she is really laughing. I haven't heard her laugh like this for ages.

"What's so funny?" I ask.

"Oh, Jackie. You. You're funny. You sure are a dark horse. Who ever would've thought you'd be such a little sneak? What else have you done that I don't know about?"

Is this my mother's way of trying to get me to confess about my father and Nicole? She must suspect something. It isn't natural that every Sunday I come home and pretend we've done nothing but sit in his basement bachelor apartment watching feet go by.

I know the best way to do it. A picture's worth a thousand words, right? I stand up and unzip my jeans. Then I pull down the band of my underpants and reveal the butterfly. I'm glad now that I never showed it to Nicole. I'm glad my mother will get to see it before her.

"Jackie! Where'd you get that?"

"Nicole gave it to me."

"And who is Nicole?"

"You mean you really don't know?"

"No, but I can guess. I know your father has a girlfriend. I've known for a long time. Is that her name?" I just nod my head. I'm so embarrassed.

"It's not your fault, Jackie. Anyway, I've suspected for ages that you must be seeing her. You're always pretty secretive about what you've done on Sundays."

"Why didn't you ever ask?"

"Because I didn't want you to think you had to spy. I don't want you to be torn between us, Jackie. It's up to your father to tell me these things, not you. One day we'll get to the point where we can talk to each other again. It'll just take time."

I'm glad she doesn't ask me more about Nicole, about her age and what she looks like. I'd feel really bad describing her to my mother. I'd have to confess that she's tall and slim, perfectly tanned, with long blond hair and deep blue eyes and dimples. But then again, I wonder if Nicole will look as good in twenty years as my mother's looking these days?

Then I remember the starfish set. I was hoping to wear it to my first day of Grade 9 next week. I was thinking I'd have to carry it to school in my knapsack and put it on there. I couldn't risk her seeing it and then having to explain who bought it for me. I remember how Nicole brushed my hair to the side to fasten it, her breath right on my neck. The way she really seemed pleased by how much I liked it and how good it looked on me. I still find Nicole hard to hate.

I thought there was no way I could ever show the jewellery to my mother. I'd have to hide it forever. But now I'm not so sure.

"Let's order a pizza, Jackie. I'm famished."

"Sorry about the job, Mom. What will you do?"

"Don't worry. Theresa's mother just needs to cool down. She's under a lot of stress right now. Besides, it'll be nice to have some time off. You start back to school next week and we haven't done anything together. I've been too preoccupied, I think. I should say sorry to you."

Then she gets up to order the pizza. When I hear her ask for extra cheese, I think this day has really turned out all right after all.

Chapter 24

My mother and I do a lot of things together during the rest of that week, my last one of freedom before school starts. We go shopping for clothes, have our hair cut, and see a matinee showing of the second Lord of the Rings, *The Two Towers*.

Every time we leave to catch the bus, we look over at Theresa's house. Its stone front is so cold and silent. It doesn't give any clue about what's going on inside. My mother keeps wanting to call and see how Theresa is, but then she decides it's best to give the family their space. They may be dealing with some pretty heavy news. I've been consoling myself with thoughts of Theresa showing her angel off to the nurses and other sick kids. Somehow, I don't think it would have been that easy to wash off right away. Its colours were really deep, especially the blue of the wings.

Then, on Saturday afternoon, Theresa's mother calls. I answer the phone. She isn't overly friendly to me, but she doesn't sound hostile, either. I wait for her to tell me that Theresa misses our visits, but she doesn't. It's my mother she wants to speak to. I sit at the kitchen table and try to eavesdrop, but it's hard to tell what's being said because all my mother keeps saying is "uh-huh, I see" over and over again. Then she hangs up. When she swivels toward me I see she's smiling. "It's great news, Jackie. They did all kinds of tests on Theresa and she seems to be getting better and stronger. They think it may be signs of remission, but it's still a bit early to tell."

My mother then goes on about blood cells and leukocytes and anemia and other scientific terms. She sounds like she's reciting a textbook, and I can suddenly see her back in college, top of her class, memorizing technical terms. When she says "medical miracle," my ears shut off. I don't think it was a miracle at all. There isn't any medical mumbo-jumbo that my mother can throw at me to try to explain it all. When I imagine Theresa, I see the colourful angel on her arm, soaring above the white cloudy pillows into the air.

I know exactly what saved her.

"Are you going to start working there again?" I ask. I cross my fingers behind my back, hoping she'll say no. My mother's been so focused on me this week, I don't want her to go back to the way she was.

"You know, Jackie. I've been thinking about taking some nursing courses, real nursing courses. I think we can do it. Your father's being pretty generous with money." Should I go wash out my ears? My mother just said something positive about my father.

Later that day, I decide to just go over and see Theresa for myself. What's the point in sitting around guessing? If I'd hesitated about the tattoo, I would never have done it. One thing this summer has taught me is that I have to start listening to myself. If I'd done that, I never would have allowed Katie to talk me into going to that stupid party. Katie and I still haven't spoken. It's going to make going back to school pretty awkward. I'm sure to see her there. She'll be surrounded by her gang, probably passing around the pictures of Tod.

"Jackie?" Theresa's mother is totally surprised to see me.

"I'd really like to see Theresa. Please. I promise I won't do anything outrageous. See? I have nothing with me." I hold up my arms as though she's a cop about to frisk me. I'm surprised when she finds this amusing and actually laughs.

"Well, I know Theresa would want to see you. So ... okay. She's in her room." I expected to find Theresa on her bed, in her nightgown. But she isn't. She's dressed like a normal teenager, in jeans and a T-shirt.

"Wow! You look fantastic," I say.

"Thanks. I feel good. The doctor told my mother she has to let me out of bed more if she wants me to get stronger. Even if I just get dressed and walk around the house."

"That's great. You'll be back in school before you know it."

"I don't know about that. I've never gone to school here, you know. It would be weird. I'd probably be put back a year, if not two."

"Whatever! If you go to my school we can walk together." A new idea hits me like a thunderbolt. Didn't the doctor say she needed to get up and about more? And didn't I promise to start paying more attention to that voice in my head?

"Want to practise?" I ask.

"Practise what?"

"Walking to school. It's not far, just one long and one short block past where we went last time. You can do it. And it's not as hot out today. And we'll bring water."

"Okay, I guess." We fill two empty bottles with water in the kitchen and I make Theresa put on a sun hat.

"There's one last thing we need. We should tell your mother first," I say. "It would probably be better if you tell her." Theresa calls her mother down from upstairs.

"Mom, Jackie wants to take me for a short walk. Remember how the doctor said it would be good for me to start getting around more?" Theresa's mother shoots me this look as if to say she shouldn't have trusted me. "It was my idea, not Jackie's," Theresa lies. "I want to do it."

"Well … okay, but don't go far, and I want you back in an hour at the latest."

"Don't worry, Mrs. Desjardins. I'll look out for her," I say. I'm just about to add, "like last time," but catch myself. I loop my arm into Theresa's and we take it slowly. I'm just praying that my mother won't see us from across the street, but I wonder if she'd run out and try to stop us anyway? Theresa stops to drink water every so often and I join her. When we get to the caterpillar hedge we peek inside, but there aren't any orange stripes this time. At the corner, I have to decide whether to turn right now and then left, or to keep going and turn right at the next corner. The school is right there. The main difference is that if we turn right then left, we'll be walking up Katie's street.

"Let's turn right here, then we'll go up the next block. It's got more shade," I say. But I'm not sure that's the real reason I want to go this way.

I can see the roof of Katie's house over the tops of some pine trees. Was it really only a week ago that I sat on her bed, listening to her describe Tod, letting her assure me that she'd save me from the mess I'd made of this summer?

I hadn't planned to do this, but at the foot of Katie's walkway, I turn to Theresa and say, "I want my friend Katie to meet you. We'll only stop for a minute. Is that okay?" Theresa doesn't say no, and once again I get the feeling she's just too used to being told what to do. She'll have to learn to make her own decisions as she gets stronger, especially if she wants to survive high school. I'm glad she'll have me there to look out for her, if this really is a remission. My mother said that it's too early to tell, officially.

"Jackie!" Hard to believe, but Katie looks caught off guard when she opens the door. Spontaneity isn't something she's fond of. She likes to plan events. This is the first time I've just dropped in on her in five years of friendship.

"Hi, Katie. I just wanted you to meet Theresa." My arm is still looped into Theresa's, so she is standing right beside me. "Remember I told you we'd become friends?"

"Yeah. Sure." Katie doesn't even look at Theresa. She kind of reminds me of how uncomfortable I used to be with Theresa, at the beginning of summer, before she became real to me.

"And another thing I want to do is tell you that I didn't appreciate you up there dancing with Alex and his girlfriend, like nothing was wrong, at the party last Saturday. It was really insensitive."

Katie's mouth falls open. Then, like a limp balloon being filled with air, she gathers strength and stands taller. "Well, Jackie, it's not my fault you take everything so seriously. You know you need to learn to lighten up. That's probably why Alex dumped you in the first place." I remember her saying pretty much the same thing to me when I told her my parents had split up, that I needed to lighten up about it. She has no clue. Maybe nothing bad has ever happened to her, so she's never been tested. I find myself viciously hoping that Nova Scotia loverboy dumps her long distance.

Let's see how lightly she'd take that.

"You don't know what you're talking about, Katie. And another thing — you make a lousy friend. You wouldn't know how to show compassion to anyone. All you care about is looking good." I say it quickly, then spin on my heels so that Katie doesn't have time to react. Theresa is forced to spin with me. I feel Katie's eyes boring holes into my back. As we walk away, I think how I'll have to start from scratch at school on Monday. I'll have to build a new circle of friends. But that's okay. I'll know what I'm looking for this time.

We continue up the street toward the school. Theresa is really quiet. I wonder what she thinks of Katie. She seems to be smiling in a funny way.

"Was that really your best friend?" Theresa asks finally, as we step through the gates onto school property.

"Well, yeah. At least, I thought she was. Why?"

"'Cause. If she was your friend, I'd hate to meet your enemies."

I don't know why, but this strikes me as really funny, maybe even the funniest thing I've heard all summer. I slip my arm out from under Theresa's and cover my face with my hands. Then I laugh. It starts off low, then, when I remember that there's absolutely no one here to hear me, I remove my hands and really crack up. The high brick wall of the school is like an echo chamber, and soon my high cackle is bouncing off the walls like a tennis ball. Theresa is just watching me, her eyes open wide. She's probably thinking that I'm a complete lunatic. But when I look at her I notice an expression of deep concentration on her face, which is cocked to the side. Then she closes her eyes but continues to lift her face, as though she's following something in her mind. Suddenly, she opens her mouth and lets out a couple of high-pitched hoots.

"Wow!" she says. "Great acoustics." Then Theresa opens her mouth wide once again and releases the most amazing scale. She starts low and rises to such a high note that I think I see the glass in the windows vibrate. She has an awesome voice. She's still holding that last note, belting it out like an opera singer. Theresa the soprano. Finally she stops, then sings the scale in reverse. On the final low note, her chin collapses onto her neck. She looks exhausted and ecstatic all at once.

"Do you need to sit down?" I ask. She nods and I lead her to a picnic bench. "You really need to join the school choir, if you end up coming here, Theresa. Your voice is amazing."

"I know, I told you I could sing."

"Let's do it together," I say. "One, two, three." Then we both belt out the scale. Her voice soars way higher than mine, but mine's in there, kind of floating under hers. The echo is incredible. It's like we are a whole choir. It's amazing how free I feel with nobody here, like I could do or say anything. I know that when the school is filled with people next week, especially Katie and her gang and Alex and his friends, I won't feel this way. But maybe remembering today will help me cope.

"Hey, Jackie. I haven't shown it to you yet."

"What?"

"My tattoo." Theresa rolls up her sleeve and reveals the angel. It's still pretty bright. How is that possible?

"I wouldn't let anyone wash my arm," Theresa says. "Not even at the hospital. I made them take all my blood from my other arm, and in the shower I wrapped it in a towel and held it outside the water. Can you believe it?"

"You're amazing, Theresa." I remember how, earlier in the summer, I thought Theresa didn't have any fighting spirit. I thought she was just too resigned to her situation, that if she fought against all the restrictions, she'd be able to do more. But now I know I was wrong. She was simply smart enough to know what she could and couldn't fight.

In spite of being sick, Theresa knew herself better than I knew myself.

There are some things I have to accept — like my parents no longer being together, and my father being with Nicole. But there are other things I can change — like who I choose to be friends with. Or girlfriends with.

It's funny, but I don't feel like a fragile tooth-pick bridge that has collapsed anymore. I did at first, when I knew I'd blown it with Alex. Instead, I feel pretty strong.

Strong enough to get Theresa all this way and back. We don't take Katie's street on the way home. I don't need her to see Theresa again. We're still moving pretty slowly, but Theresa isn't withering. She's holding up.

In fact, between her blue wings and my red and green ones, I think we could fly home if we wanted to.